DEPUTY'S JOB . . .

Shamrock slid out of the saddle and started through the gate. He was ten feet into the corral when a shot from the bunkhouse kicked dirt at his feet.

"Tell the sheriff to come along!" a voice called from inside.

Shamrock did not even pause in his lazy, casual, self-assured stride. The second shot was closer still. From the four windows of the bunkhouse, eight rifles pointed at him.

"Go back and send Sheriff Lobell!"

Still Shamrock came on. He was sweating a little. The end rifle cracked, and Shamrock felt something tug at his shirt.

He looked down and saw a hole in his shirt low at his side near his waistline. Still he walked on.

"Stop right there!"

THE MAN ON THE BLUE

Luke Short

A Dell Book

Published by
DELL PUBLISHING CO., INC.
1 Dag Hammarskjold Plaza
New York, N.Y. 10017

ISBN: 0-440-15255-0

Printed in the United States of America
Previous Dell Editions #31, A151, 5255
New Dell Edition
First printing—April 1978

CHAPTER ONE

"I'M NOT THEENK THAT RIGHT. Here. I'm show you."

The Mexican reached for the cactus stick being used as a pointer by his companion. When he had it, he suddenly realized that he alone was holding it, that his companion had let go, had stepped away.

He looked up.

"Go on," his companion said. "Only be careful how you reach out that way again."

The Mexican hefted the stick, and was about to speak, then changed his mind and walked the twenty feet to the top of the ridge. There the wind caught his ragged clothes, whipping faint streamers of alkali dust out behind him, molding them against his heavy, squat body, even stirring the low-slung gun at his thigh.

"She's come close," he said. "Twenty, maybe." His companion said nothing, and the Mexican returned. He pointed the stick at a rough map drawn in the sand drift in the lee of the ridge. The map was a big square cut in fours, and he placed the stick almost where the lines intersected.

"I'm theenk we are here."

"Still in Colorado?"

"*Si.*"

"Not far in."

"Not far." The Mexican's swart face turned and his gaze shuttled to the two horses standing hipshot down the face of the ridge a dozen yards away. His eyes were harried, filled with unease, as they settled on the map again, and he moved the stick to the upper left-hand square.

"Utah Terr'tory," he said, looking at his companion.

"No good. They want me."

The Mexican moved the stick to the opposite lower square.

"*Nuevo Mejico.*"

"Speak English."

"New Mexico Terr'tory."

"No. They want me, too."

The frustration in the Mexican's eyes was eloquent as he looked at his companion.

The man stood well away from the map, so that he appeared little concerned with it. He was not tall, not heavy, either, but close-knit. As he stood there with his hands on his hips, his narrow, small fingers playing loosely over the gun belt sagging from his hip, his arrogance was regal. His clothes were ordinary—the drab blue shirt and Levi's of the workaday range variety now covered with alkali dust— and so was his well-worn cedar-handled Colt, his saddle-softened half boots. It was his face.

It was small, oval, still, cold, browned to the color of oak leaves at first frost, and smooth; his eyes were rain-gray, and had the opacity of slate, the surface lights of agate. Half the upper lip of his rather generous mouth was lifted in a sneer, stamped that way from habit. He stood so straight and still that he contrived more than poise. It was a quality of gathering explosiveness, rather. He wore his arrogance like a banner—and a proud one.

"*Por Dios,*" the Mexican muttered, his gaze beaten down. "Them posse, she's wanting us in Colorado now. W'at is left?"

Then, as if it reminded him of his duty, he walked to the top of the ridge and looked off toward the northeast.

"She's come closer. She's more than twenty."

His companion said nothing, and he returned to the map.

"I'm theenk only Arizona Terr'tory left."

"What's it like?"

The Mexican made a quick, loose gesture of impatience with his hand. "Them posse, she's close."

"What's it like?"

The Mexican sighed and said rapidly, "*Mucho calor—* veree hot. Long rides weeth no water. Them country, she's up and down. She's got small horses, but mean. No grass, no water, and them *ranchos,* she's many days ride between. She's no good."

"Towns?"

"She's not many."

Again the Mexican interrupted himself to go to the top of the ridge. Once there, he looked, started to squat in a rapid, serpentlike movement, then rose slowly and cursed. He said to his companion, "There. She's see me sure."

Slowly his companion drew a Durham sack from his shirt pocket and in no particular haste rolled and lighted a smoke, looking off over the country to the south. The Mexican watched him.

"I think I'll try it."

The Mexican exhaled his breath sharply. "Then *adios,* Señor Shamrock. In Arizona, they want me t'ree t'ousand dollars wort'. Me, I'm go to Utah."

He looked at his companion a long moment, then slowly added, "Some day I'm theenk you cough some sand from your craw. She's no good, them face. She's too tough not to bust."

His companion spoke around his cigarette. "Want to try it, Pablo?"

"Not I'm," the Mexican said quietly. "Me, I'm not so tough."

"Then drag it."

"*Adios,* Shamrock."

"*Adios.*"

7

"And *vaya con Dios,* my fr'en. You need Heem, thees God. He loves you now, but not forever."

"Drag it."

The Mexican ran to his horse. He mounted in one agile leap, rammed home his spurs, and headed west, traveling the side of the ridge, his jaded roan already in a gallop.

Shamrock watched him a moment, then whistled. The big, bony blue down the slope wheeled and walked smartly up the hill to him.

He walked up the ridge and looked over it. Below, less than a quarter mile, he could see more than a dozen horsemen flailing their ponies up the flinty and treacherous footing of the slope. They saw him, for a puff of smoke folded out from the leader of the group, the dirt geysered up a score of yards down the ridge, then the slap of the shot sounded.

He swung lazily onto the blue, settled the old and battered Stetson more securely over his blue-black hair, and was picking up his reins when he caught sight of the map in the sand. He dismounted, again lazily, and with a half-dozen dragging motions of his booted foot, he erased the map.

Then he mounted and turned in the saddle. There were more shots now, many of them close. With a careless gesture of insolence, he raised a hand in salute to the posse, and started down the ridge.

By the time the posse had reached the top of the ridge, he was out of sight, headed south and a little west into the canyon country below that was blazing red in the last light of windy day.

Just over the ridge, the posse drew up, and the leader dismounted. Two others followed him, and they studied the tracks, walking down the slope.

"They've split," one man said.

"Which is the biggest tracks?" the leader, an elderly

man with a seamed, hard-bitten face, asked.

"Them goin' south."

"That'll be him," the leader said. "Let that Mex go."
He looked off to the south, swearing softly.

"The line ain't far," one man said wearily.

"They can have him," the leader said bitterly, passionately. "I hope he rides into somethin' there—somethin'
that will wipe that damn sneer off'n his face. I hope he
does."

"He won't."

The leader sighed. "No. Likely he won't." He turned
up the slope again. "Well, let's go. We can make damn
certain we're rid of him, anyway."

CHAPTER TWO

THAT WAS WEDNESDAY. Since then he had been riding
doggedly for the blue bulk of the Santa Ritas far to the
south. Today was Tuesday. During all that time he could
count on one hand the number of times his blue had drunk.
He had drunk half that many himself, but now that he was
approaching the Santa Rita foothills he was reasonably
sure his thirst would soon end.

He had counted on it, anyway, counted on it for almost
a week. Where there were mountains, there was grazing,
and where there was grazing, there must be water. Right—
but where was it?

At noon he had crossed a trail that seemed to flank the
foothills, a trail wagons had been over recently. He had
taken it, after considering the country, for a team here
wouldn't venture far from water.

But by midafternoon he was debating whether to leave

the trail and hit straight for the mountains to the west. It wouldn't be long before his tongue started swelling from thirst, and this trail seemed to be winding interminably into dry arroyos, skirting rocky, cedar-covered ridges, traversing the same country with dreary, dry monotony. He looked out over the country to the east with a wry distaste in his face. It sheered off on a dozen different planes, each plane a different color until the blue of utter distance blotted it together. There was no grass on it, and it held the blacks and reds and rusts and purples of malpais and rock—rock eternally. It looked as bleak and dry to a man just fresh from the short-grass country as the whitened skeleton of a beef. Only the Santa Ritas, high, green, aloof, immediately beyond the foothills to the west, looked at all inviting.

He reined up on the heel of a ridge and regarded them. They were far, even though they looked close. A glance at the endless dry hills ahead about decided him, when he looked closer. Yes, off there to the south was a small blotch of light green thrusting over a ridge. It was the unmistakable color of cottonwood foliage—and that meant water.

With a barely audible sigh of relief he wheeled the blue back into the trail and rode on in the somnolent mantle of dry heat.

When he felt his weight settle back in the saddle several minutes later, he looked ahead. He was climbing the ridge of the hump where he could see the cottonwoods. The blue pricked up his ears.

Then, topping the rise, he reined up sharply, jolted out of his midafternoon drowse.

There, thirty yards beyond, heading for some rocks past the cottonwood trees, was a rider mounted on a big chestnut. At the end of a lariat dallied from the saddle horn, a man was dragging.

Shamrock could see that the dust-covered victim was

unconscious and unable to struggle, and he knew that it was only a matter of seconds before the rider's chestnut would drag him into the distant rocks.

Instinctively Shamrock spurred his blue into a gallop, heading for the dragged man. Whipping out his knife, he leaned out of the saddle and as he reached the lariat he cut it.

The chestnut, freed of the dragging weight, almost stumbled. The rider yanked up the chestnut's head, and then turned in the saddle.

Shamrock had reined up now and pulled out his gun.

"Don't," he said, his gun leveled and cocked.

Then he saw: a girl.

Her first shot was wide, but Shamrock didn't wait. He rolled out of his saddle and in the same motion sprawled behind a rock at the side of the road.

"Come out of there!" a girl's voice, furious and shrill, called. Another shot slapped into the rock. Shamrock took off his Stetson, laid it over his up-tilted gun, then, while he edged his head around the far end of the rock into a clump of screening mesquite, he eased his Stetson over the top of the rock.

She was dismounted now, he saw; and when she caught sight of the Stetson, she opened up again, three times in rapid succession. When she was finished, Shamrock stood up.

"Put it down," he said coldly.

It took him a couple of seconds to rightly understand the girl's intent. Then he saw that she wasn't putting it down, that she was feverishly trying to reload her gun.

Leaping over the rock, he raced toward her. Ten feet away, he heard the loading gate of her Colt click shut, saw it begin to swing up—and he dived.

They went down in a slamming moil of dust, Shamrock fighting for her gun wrist and twisting the Colt free. He got up, stood over her, breathing a little hard, his head bare, the dust motes settling on his blue-black hair.

He heard the sucking, gasping breaths as she raised herself to one knee, head hung. She was getting her wind. All he could see of her was a loose mass of mahogany-colored hair and he backed off a little, his face still, his eyes wary.

When she looked up at him, the first thing he noticed was the fury in her green eyes that seemed to dominate everything else, the small compact face with its freckled, up-tilted nose, its generous mouth with now bloodless lips.

"So you're another," she blazed.

"No."

"You fool! If it hadn't been for you he'd be dead!"

Shamrock watched her coldly a moment. "Why should he?"

"Why should he? You stand there and ask that!" she said savagely. "You're another of his hired gunmen, and you pretend you don't know!"

She stood up to him now, and was half a head shorter than he. Her dress was a rough riding suit of dark gray over which she wore a man's gun belt that sagged heavily at her waist.

Shamrock plugged the shells from her gun and gave it to her, his face sneering.

"Get out. Get clear out."

She grabbed the gun and as soon as she had it, she started to load it again. He laid a hand on the gun, holding it steady against her tugging.

"Listen," he said. "I don't like women. I don't like you. Get out before I forget you wear a skirt."

With a swift, vicious back-draw of her arm, she slapped his face. It cracked loudly in the stillness of the afternoon and he stood perfectly still a second, his hand still on the gun. Then he wrenched the Colt from her in a sweeping movement that kited it far behind him, stooped, gathered her up in his arms and strode over to her horse. Once there, he pitched her over the saddle, face down, looped the reins over her chestnut's head, and gave him a cut across the rump. The horse rocketed up in a half-rear, then skitted out and stretched into a run. She was still on, hand braced in the stirrup, when she disappeared over the ridge.

He raised a hand to his stinging face and rubbed it gently as he turned to look at the unconscious man. He was lying on his side, back to Shamrock, hands bound behind him. Even so, Shamrock could see he was a big man and middle-aged, for his hair was almost white. His black pants were tucked in half boots, and he wore a vest over a blue shirt. Off forty yards down the road, the man's horse stood looking over his shoulder at Shamrock. There was a canteen on the saddle, and Shamrock made for that first, looking curiously at the man's broad back as he passed.

It was an effort to refrain from taking the canteen the first thing and drinking it dry, but he unslung it and walked back to the man, his curiosity almost as strong as his thirst. Laying the canteen on the ground, he untied the man's bonds, then rolled him over on his back.

The first thing that caught his eye was the star of the sheriff's office pinned on the man's vest. Shamrock straightened slowly, looked fleetingly in the direction the girl's horse had taken, then looked back at the sheriff.

"I shouldn't have done that," he said aloud. "No, sir, I shouldn't have done that."

The sheriff's face was just losing some of its red flush. It was a broad, open face, rather kind and worn, with slight jowls that gave it the gentle aspect of a hound dog's in repose.

With a soft curse, Shamrock picked up the canteen, unscrewed the top, and was about to drink from it when he looked over at his horse. Blue was watching him with pointed ears, his thirst eloquent.

Resolutely, Shamrock lowered the canteen and looked down at the sheriff, distaste reflected on his still face. Then he held the canteen out at arm's length about four feet above the sheriff's face and tilted it. The pouring was not very accurate at that distance, but after some slight maneuvering he got the stream regulated so the water hit the sheriff squarely in his half-open mouth. It was a game, and he concentrated on it with childish relish, his face insolent and hard and faintly amused. Suddenly the sheriff coughed, and he ceased pouring.

He threw the canteen to the ground, backed off a few feet, and squatted on his heels, rolling a cigarette.

The sheriff sat up slowly. He was rubbing his neck when he first saw Shamrock, and he observed him with amiable blue eyes. He wiped the water from his face with a shirt sleeve.

"You cut me loose."

Shamrock nodded. "It was a mistake."

The sheriff's face changed only a trifle, but his eyes became a little more shrewd. "Where's the water?"

Shamrock nodded to the canteen midway between them, but made no effort to get it. The sheriff understood, and he hoisted himself to his feet, picked up the canteen, and drank, then offered it to Shamrock.

He shook his head. The sheriff, without saying anything, reached in his upper vest pocket and, from a brown paper sack whose top peeped over the pocket edge, he extracted a round, white peppermint drop and slipped it into his mouth. He maneuvered it into his cheek, and began to suck, still regarding Shamrock.

"Which way'd you come from?"

"North."

"Then maybe your horse would like the rest of this."

"He ain't thirsty, either."

The sheriff gazed at him with mild reproof. "Son, just because you don't like my looks, it's no reason to make your horse go thirsty. You've come from the north, you say. There ain't water up there in a long day's ride."

"We've drunk," Shamrock said coldly.

The sheriff shrugged and screwed the cap back on the canteen. "My name's Andy Lobell," he volunteered quietly. "I'm obliged to you for cuttin' me loose. The last I knew I was set to cash in my chips."

"Aren't women bullies?" Shamrock asked dryly.

"Which way did she go?"

The girl had gone north. Shamrock, his eyes jeering, pointed south.

The sheriff observed him steadily. "That ain't so. She'd head for the Double Diamond pronto, and it lies over that way." He pointed northwest, toward the mountains.

Shamrock said nothing, but his gray eyes were insolent, mocking, not the way a man's eyes should be when he is caught in a lie.

The sheriff caught the jeering and his jaw clicked shut with a faint snap. Erect, he was a big man, an imposing figure, and as he turned to get his horse there was a dignity in his movements that Shamrock noted with cynical acuteness.

Then he forgot the sheriff, and started looking for water. As his gaze roved the clump of cottonwoods, he was brought to the disgusting realization that there was none. Doubtless the trees were fed by an underground spring, but it did him no good. There was water in the canteen enough to wash the dust from Blue's throat and his own, but he would not have taken it. He would rather ride dry for another day.

"Which way you ridin'?" the sheriff asked. He was holding the reins of his big bay, just settling his dust-colored

Stetson on his head. Shamrock turned slowly and gave him a blank look.

"South."

"Good. I'll side you."

Shamrock had his mouth open to assert that he had meant he was riding north, but his thirst conquered. Surely the sheriff would lead him to water. He could stand the company of the old codger that long.

They mounted and headed south, Shamrock's blue keeping just a little behind the sheriff's bay as he had been trained to do.

They rode a while in silence, the sheriff obviously casting about for some way to open a pleasant conversation.

"How do you like our country?" he asked finally.

"Sheep country."

For several minutes after that the sheriff held his peace, and it suited Shamrock. He tried to forget his thirst by thinking of something else, and quite naturally his thoughts returned to the girl and her deed. Who had she taken him for?

"Dang her!" the sheriff said, as if he had been following the course of Shamrock's thought. "She's a heller, that one," he continued grimly, looking at Shamrock. "It's plumb hell when a woman gets that way. You can't fight back."

"No," Shamrock said, and the tone of his voice implied he meant just the opposite.

"Then not with her," the sheriff said, understanding the contradiction. "A ordinary little snip like that you could spank and git it over with. But her—she's Mayo Hyatt's sister."

He looked at Shamrock as if his statement explained much. Shamrock waited just long enough, then said, "Never heard of him."

"Then you sure are new to this country," the sheriff said

grimly. "In fact, you must have been keeping way wide of it and a lot of other country if you haven't heard of him."

"Never heard of him," Shamrock repeated.

"Why, hell, man," the sheriff said with unexpected bitterness. "He's that killer the governor just paroled last month. He was bein' hunted hard down south there. So he rode a Wells-Fargo stage over the Mogollons. He was disguised. The stage had a load of gold from the Smoky River field, and in one of them passes a gang stuck it up. They killed the guard, but this Hyatt fought 'em off and rolled the stage down into Globe. The governor, he has an interest in them Smoky River mines, and it was partly his gold, so he paroled him. He's here now—this Hyatt."

"Where?"

"In Malpais Springs," the sheriff said sourly. "He ain't been here a month and I'm scared to go out nights."

Shamrock shot a quick glance at the sheriff and decided immediately that his modesty was false. But the statement paved the way for an innocent question Shamrock had been wanting to ask, so he did.

"That's his name, then? Mayo Hyatt?"

The sheriff looked at him. "His real one, yes. You know him?"

"I don't know the name."

"That's funny," the sheriff drawled. "They tell me he had quite a name up there in the short-grass country."

Shamrock was drawing out his Durham sack, but he stopped. The sheriff was looking straight ahead. Had he been warned some way? Shamrock looked over his own rig, then laughed to himself. It was Blue, of course. Pablo had said they bred runty stuff down here, and Blue was big and sleek and, even after two weeks of hard riding, was not gaunted.

"I said I don't know the name," Shamrock repeated coldly.

"I heard you. But you will. It didn't take you long to hear of his sister, and if you stay in Malpais Springs or even Jicarilla County very long, you'll hear of him."

Shamrock finished the cigarette and lighted it, his face hard. He was certain now that the sheriff was feeling for something, saying things hit or miss, taking contradictions as they came—and meanwhile finding out about everything he wanted to know about Shamrock.

So Shamrock inhaled deeply and said, "Listen, Pop. My name is Shamrock—Shamrock Ireland. You don't know me. You never will. I'm ridin' through this country as fast as this blue will take me—straight through. I don't give a damn about this Hyatt. I don't even give half a damn about his sister. And I don't even give half of a half of a damn about your county feuds. Savvy?"

The sheriff reined up and wheeled his horse across the road. Shamrock had already checked Blue, and their horses stood side by side. Shamrock's hand nearest the sheriff was resting on his thigh. His eyes were mocking, hard.

"Maybe you'd like this road to yourself," the sheriff said.

"Maybe I would."

"All right. Take it. First, though, I'll ask my questions."

"Get it over."

"It may take time."

"Get it over."

"All right. These Hyatts—Mayo and his sister Nancy—have lost their spread, the Double Diamond, to the bank. While Mayo was away with the Wild Bunch, Nancy run it into the ground. It's time to foreclose. But when Mayo gets home, he says the first man that serves a paper on him better serve it with a gun. He claims every nester and small rancher in the county helped hisself to Double Diamond beef while he was away, and that he's hanged if he'll give the spread up." He shrugged. "The papers have gone through legal—but there ain't a man in the county that will serve the dispossess notice on him."

"Why don't you?"

"Not me," Lobell said. "I'm scared of him. He'd cut me to doll rags. Nancy hates me so danged much that she followed me out of town this mornin' and—well, you seen it."

"Get to it."

"I want to deputize you and have you serve the dispossess notice." He raised a hand before Shamrock could answer. "There's five hundred dollars in it for the man that serves it. After that—a posse'll do the rest. I want it to be legal—airtight. Will you do it?"

"No," Shamrock said promptly.

"Why not?"

"When I hire out to counter-jumpers, it won't be to a bank."

The smile on the sheriff's face was resigned. "I thought so. It looked too danged good to be true." He pulled his horse off into the wayside *chamisa* and waited for Shamrock to pass. Shamrock did not move.

"You thought what?"

"With that face, a man ought to be tough enough to back it up. That's all. Go on."

Quickly Shamrock slid out of the saddle and walked over toward the sheriff.

He flipped his gun to the ground and stood a few feet away from it.

"Pick it up or shut up."

"Not me," the sheriff said evenly. "I'm almost an old man. I never claimed to throw a gun. I know a stuffed Stetson when I see one, though."

Where the sheriff's jibe would have angered another man to fury, it served to calm Shamrock. He knew the sheriff was no coward and that his taunting was no prelude to a gun fight. Shamrock had put it squarely to him, and Lobell had refused. Then there was some other reason, a private reason, that Shamrock could not understand.

"What's the game?" he asked warily.

The sheriff's eyes were steady and challenging as he answered, "You got it—face up. Five hundred to serve a paper on a gunman."

"What else?"

The sheriff hesitated before he answered, "Nothin'. You'll have the law behind you."

Which was to say that if anyone—Hyatt, for instance—was killed, there would be no questions asked. That accounted for the price, too.

"So that's it," Shamrock said softly. "I get paid a thousand dollars for goin' up against a gunman and I won't have to run if I down him."

"Five hundred," the sheriff corrected.

"A thousand."

"All right," Lobell said immediately. He reached into his pocket and drew out something which he tossed to Shamrock. Shamrock did not even look at it, did not try to catch it. He knew it was a deputy's badge. It fell in the road and lay there as he mounted Blue.

"Not if I have to wear that damn thing."

"I thought so," the sheriff said amiably, chuckling a little.

CHAPTER THREE

MALPAIS SPRINGS was tucked so deep in a fold of the Santa Rita foothills that its sunrise was later, its sunset earlier than seemed probable to a man viewing it from the hills. It squatted on the south bank of a dry stream bed, and was served by a long if unsubstantial bridge that opened onto its main four corners.

Otherwise, the town had a thousand duplicates in the west. False-front stores faced each other across a wide and dusty street. Wooden awnings shaded most of the footage of boardwalk that was flanked by hitchracks. Lamps were just being lighted for the night, and while the town could not be described as a boom town, there was activity on the streets, saddle horses and buckboards at the racks which denoted that it was the seat of a prosperous cattle country.

The sheriff, who had been content with the silence that fell between them, pointed ahead to a squat board shack on the corner.

"That there's the office. Come in and I'll get the paper."

"I'll be in tomorrow."

"Where do you aim to put up?"

"I don't know. I'll be in tomorrow."

Without waiting for a reply, Shamrock turned down left on the main street. He had seen the big bulk of the livery stable from the hill, and he made for it, not even looking back at the sheriff who had stopped and was regarding him with a grim annoyance.

At the huge door of the livery stable above which was proclaimed *Hay & Grain* on a weathered sign, Shamrock reined Blue in and dismounted stiffly.

From the dark depth of the stalls a figure with a lantern came toward him. Shamrock made out a boy, possibly sixteen, who approached, whistling.

"Yes, *sir*," he announced cheerfully, looking at Blue before he did Shamrock. He was gangly, all elbows and knees and hands, and his clothes were unbelievably ragged and patched, though clean. His boots were mismatched, both as to size and make, and he had the legs of his soft Levi's tucked in them. An upstanding shock of blond hair, a pair of wide, curious hazel eyes now studying Blue with silent admiration, and a wide mouth screwed up to accommodate an off-key whistle made up his features.

"He ain't the first horse I've had to nurse after makin' a half-dozen dry camps," he announced importantly. "Easy does it."

Then he looked at Shamrock, resuming his whistling. The whistling died abruptly.

"Double grain him when he's cooled off," Shamrock said. "And go easy on that water."

"Yes, sir," the lad said humbly. He led Blue back into the first stall, and Shamrock followed him. The youngster started to work, good-naturedly fighting Blue away from the water bucket, but letting him have a sip now and then. Shamrock watched him and was satisfied.

"What's your name?" Shamrock asked.

"Maginnis."

Shamrock rolled a cigarette and regarded the youngster's work.

"Put that saddle on the manger," he ordered suddenly. "I may want to leave here in a hurry."

Again the youngster obeyed, and he was not whistling any more.

Shamrock lighted up, scowling. "Does this Hyatt have red hair?" he asked suddenly.

Maginnis looked up. "Mighty red."

"A big man, almost thirty, with a scar on his left cheek?"

"That's him," Maginnis said.

"Gunman?"

"Looks it."

Shamrock flipped a couple of silver dollars on the floor where Maginnis was kneeling. "That's for you. I'll settle my bill later."

"Yes, sir," the boy said softly. "They won't get nothin'

out of me."

Shamrock was half turned to go when he paused and looked at Maginnis again.

"Who won't?"

"Why—why—anybody that asks if you was inquirin' about Mayo Hyatt."

Shamrock removed the cigarette from his mouth. "Like who?"

The youngster flushed, and his gaze fell under Shamrock's cold stare. "Well, the sheriff he asks regular since Hyatt come home." He jerked his head in the direction of the sheriff's office. "Two men he tried to deputize come in here askin' me about Hyatt."

"Did he do it?"

"I—I heard they wouldn't take it," Maginnis said.

Shamrock put the cigarette back in his mouth. "All right. Where can I get a drink of water?"

"Right in my room past the office."

Shamrock went up to the office, through it in the dark to the cubbyhole beyond, which contained a cot and a washstand and not much else.

He found the bucket and filled the dipper, rinsed out his mouth, spat out a mouthful, then started to drink in short sips, waiting between each one. At the first trickle of water down his throat, everything that had been tight in him seemed to loosen up, and he suddenly discovered that he had been hungry too.

"A lawman," he suddenly said aloud, contemptuously, and laughed quietly. He was thinking of his meeting with the sheriff, and the innocent proposition he had accepted —a proposition which carried unspoken meanings they both understood. Shamrock hadn't been entirely sure until Maginnis had said it, then he knew that Lobell was on the lookout for a hardcase—any hardcase—to do a dirty job.

And he hadn't been sure about Hyatt, either, until Maginnis had verified the description Shamrock had not dared to ask Lobell. Which only went to prove, he reflected as he set the dipper down in the bucket, that everything comes to a man with patience—even Mayo Hyatt.

Still thirsty, he stepped to the door and looked over the town. It had the lonely quietness of dusk about it, and he could smell damp dirt, as if the stream bed behind the opposite buildings had not long been dry and still held the lingering freshness of mountain water. It was on just such a night as this in spring, and about this time, too, that he and Hyatt had made their deal.

In that Idaho town near the Calicos—what was its— Cosmos, that was it, he thought peacefully. *He was travelin' under the name of Hyatt Mayo then. That's what threw me off.* He could even think of it now without a red rage welling up in him.

He'd been young then, and green—green enough to think he could trust a man's face. And he had trusted Hyatt's. They had made the deal in the back room of Joe Manero's store in Cosmos, the seat of the county which the week before had put $2,000 on his and Hyatt's heads. Hyatt had been a stranger then; they had met by chance up in the hills. Both of them were on the dodge, Hyatt heading a bunch, Shamrock on his own.

Hyatt had called the meeting. It was simple enough. He wanted to pull out of the country—alone; but before he went there was a last job. It needed a man with an iron nerve. Shamrock was the man. Did Shamrock ever notice that on Friday nights the six mines around Cosmos brought their bullion in to deposit at the Cattleman's Trust and got their Saturday payrolls? Did he know that at six o'clock there was more hard cash and gold in Cosmos than one man could carry away?

Here was the plan. The sweeper at the bank could be

bought. Hyatt had bought him. The sweeper would hide Shamrock in the basement of the bank on Thursday night. Friday night, when the guarded buckboard from the Esmerelda mine rolled into town, Hyatt's gang would stick it up just off the main street. The shots would draw off the bank guards. Shamrock would come upstairs, hold up the cashier and guards, while Hyatt placed the horses in the rear, came in the bank the back way, and scooped up the assembled cash. They would go together and be reasonably free of pursuit, since the sheriff and bank guards would be fighting off the Esmerelda stick-up.

Shamrock agreed. It went off as planned, except that the man who walked in the back door of the bank was not Hyatt. It was the sheriff, with six deputies.

Hyatt had sold him out for the reward money, and by warning the sheriff, he had got most of his own gang killed off in the raid.

The fact that Shamrock had broken jail before he ever came to trial wasn't important. He had sworn to hunt Hyatt down if it took him a lifetime. Long ago the trail had blanked out, but Shamrock hadn't forgotten.

And today he had crossed it again. When the sheriff first mentioned Hyatt's name, Shamrock suspected, and when the story of the holdup in the Mogollons was told, Shamrock knew. To the sheriff he had denied knowledge of Hyatt, because when he killed Hyatt he wanted to have his back trail covered. He had even refused the sheriff's offer at first, but when the thousand dollars was mentioned he accepted. Why not take the thousand, kill Hyatt, and use the money on the trail? It meant he could travel fast, buy fresh horses if need be, and not attract attention by sticking up a stage for money or stealing a horse.

He could kill Hyatt under the full protection of this crooked sheriff and ride off with money.

And that's the only time me and the law done each

other favors, he reflected as he stepped out into the street.

Crossing the four corners at an easy pace, Shamrock noted the saloon—*Legal Tender,* he could read across its false front—was lighted up and doing a brisk business. Down the street he could see a restaurant sign, and he made for it.

The four men seated at the counter all looked up at Shamrock as he entered, and he returned their stares without any greeting or recognition. He took the far end seat and ordered steak, potatoes, coffee, and a double order of pie from the waitress. The conversation had come to an abrupt stop as it always does when men are talking before a stranger. The first man to leave was a tall puncher who carried his flat-crowned Stetson because a dirty bandage circled his head. The others, a tough lot if Shamrock was any judge, drifted out after him.

Finished with his meal, Shamrock paid the waitress and counted the money he had left. A little over thirty dollars—half the sixty he split with Pablo that he had grabbed from the poker game which the grim Colorado sheriff had broken up so precipitously. It was enough to sit in a small poker game for a couple of hours anyway, no matter what his luck.

He loafed across the street to the Legal Tender and shouldered his way through the batwing doors. The blare of the room, the stench of tobacco smoke and alcohol hit him like a soft pillow as he entered.

It was a low-ceilinged, long room with the bar on the right side as he entered. Shamrock stopped at the door end of the bar and looked over the room. Hyatt wasn't there.

"What'll it be?" the bartender said briskly.

"Small beer."

He took his drink and worked his way through the crowd to one of the poker tables. There were three of them going, and he picked the one with the smallest limit, then stood by and watched.

There was an empty chair at the table, its back to the room, and Shamrock leaned a hand on it, watching the game.

The houseman, a thin, pale-faced man with slow, humorous eyes, looked up at him.

"Want to sit in?" he invited.

Shamrock looked over the table. There were three men playing, all punchers by their looks. He looked at the man closest the wall, a man with a grave, yet pleasant, wind-tanned face who looked about thirty.

"Not unless you'll trade seats," Shamrock said to him.

The man looked him over a moment, then his face became impassive.

"My mistake. I'm in the gun fighter's seat," he said easily, and got up.

Shamrock said, "Much obliged," and took the vacated seat, his back safely against the wall.

Luck was with Shamrock, as usual. The game was stud, but in any of the variations of poker Shamrock's natural game was a bold one. His still, cold face helped him. He was a riotous bluffer, but once let an opponent label him as one, and Shamrock would play with the shrewdness of a professional gambler. He played Indian poker, wild and daring, but he played it without the red man's fatal curiosity at wrong times. Tonight only the houseman was shrewd enough to guess his game, gauge his luck, and hold his peace. The rest piled onto him with a good-humored savageness that steadily lost them money.

They had been playing an hour when the man with the bandaged head drifted over to their table, the man Shamrock had seen in the café. The rest of the players seemed to know him, but their greetings were lukewarm.

"Can I sit in?" he asked, looking at Shamrock especially.

Shamrock nodded carelessly. The grave-faced puncher stood up and stretched.

"Take my place, Soholt," he said to the newcomer. "I'm out."

Soholt's face got ugly. "What's the matter, Scott? Don't you like the company?"

Scott laughed briefly, carelessly, and turned his pockets inside out. Then, before Soholt had a chance to say anything, walked away. But his intent had been plain enough, and Soholt sat frowning.

"This here's Hank Soholt, mister," one of the punchers said to Shamrock.

"Hiyuh," Soholt said shortly, not offering his hand.

"Poco-poco," Shamrock drawled, making no move to shake hands, either. The puncher hesitated a moment for Shamrock's name, and not getting it, said, "Let's have the deal."

From then on, Shamrock had the feeling that he was being watched all the while. Only once did he look up at Soholt, and he caught the tall puncher's gaze sliding away from his.

On the deal after that, Shamrock got an ace in the hole, and proceeded to blow up the pot on his expectations. He got a king up on the third round, but so did another player. On the last card, not a pair showed on the board, but everybody checked to Shamrock, waiting for him to start it. He bet two blues, hoping to bluff them to cover. Everyone except Soholt was scared out, but he bet four blues. Shamrock upped it, Soholt upped him, so Shamrock evened it and called. Soholt didn't have a pair, either, but he had an ace in the hole, with a jack showing. Shamrock was about to turn up his ace when he looked up at Soholt. The puncher was grinning, almost sneering. Shamrock let his card settle back and exhaled his breath a little.

"Take it," he said. The pot was big, but there would

be bigger ones, and Shamrock decided to pretend he'd been bluffing and wait for another chance when Soholt would build a bigger pot.

He sheafed his cards, turned over the face-up ones, and tossed them to the houseman. His toss was too swift, and the cards did not stay bunched, but fluttered brokenly across the table. The ace fell face up on the green felt.

Soholt saw it, and laid a big hand on it, then picked it up. He looked at Shamrock.

"That's an ace."

"Put it away," Shamrock said coldly.

Soholt slammed the card down. *"Hombre,* I don't like charity."

"That's too bad," Shamrock said, not moving.

"And specially, I don't like charity from a gunman like you, Ireland," Soholt said, rising.

"You're a dirty liar," Shamrock said flatly, not moving.

Soholt streaked for his gun.

Shamrock exploded sideways out of his chair, his hand blurring up in a flash of metal and exploding hip-high.

The first shot straightened Soholt out and rammed him back, and the second fast on the first caught his foot off the ground and slammed him flat on his back. His hand was locked around his gun butt, and he did not move. He lay there staring at the ceiling, his eyes wide; his knees raising in slight jerks. Both shots had caught him in the face.

Shamrock's back was against the wall. "Anybody want to take it up?" His gun covered the room.

Someone in front of the loose circle stirred, and Shamrock swiveled his gun to cover the movement. Then the sheriff broke through and strode over to Soholt and looked down at him.

"Damn fool," Lobell said quietly.

"I'm walkin' out of here," Shamrock said. "Clear away from that bar—you swampers, too."

"He's clear," the houseman volunteered to the sheriff. "Soholt rawhided him until he had to."

"Self-defense," the sheriff pronounced.

But Shamrock nosed up his gun. "Clear away from that bar like I said."

In shuffling silence the men at the bar crossed to the other side of the room, the barkeeps following.

Then Shamrock moved slowly and carefully along the wall to the bar, traveled behind it to the far end, came out into the room, backed up against the front wall, then pivoted out the door.

He ran swiftly across the street, reached the far sidewalk, suddenly stopped, and lounged against the corner of the building, like any idle watcher.

The talk from the Legal Tender swelled out into the night in a noisy hubbub, but Shamrock waited. He saw a man come out of the saloon, look up the street toward the feed stable, then start across the street at a fast walk.

Shamrock waited until he had crossed, then swung in behind him.

They traveled that way until they reached the stables where the sheriff walked in the yawning door. A lantern stood on the floor near by and the sheriff called, "McKinley! McKinley!"

Shamrock stepped through the door behind him. "I'm still here," he said quietly.

The sheriff whirled, the startled look washing out of his face as he turned. He reached in his vest pocket, took out a peppermint drop, and slipped it into his mouth, then grunted.

"Well, if you ain't spooky," he said amiably.

"Talk," Shamrock said coldly.

"What about? Soholt?"

"He called me Ireland," Shamrock said. "A gunman, too. Been talkin'?"

"I haven't spoke your name," Lobell said quietly.

"How'd he know?"

"They still print reward posters," Lobell said gently.

Shamrock's eyes did not change, but he felt his body tense.

"Not about me."

The sheriff nodded. "A nice one—about that marshal in Billings. Three thousand for you—dead or alive."

Shamrock backed off slowly, his hands on his belt. It must be so, for Lobell could not have found out about the marshal any other way.

"Well?" he said softly.

The sheriff laughed easily. "Danged if you ain't spooky. I don't want you. Take it easy."

Shamrock scowled. "Who knows me here, Lobell? That marshal was a crook that went for his gun when I caught him cheatin' in a card game. They don't send reward posters clear down here over that."

"With your record, son, you should know by now that a Federal killin' is advertised in all the Territories."

"Town marshal," Shamrock said.

"Huh-uh. Deputy U.S. He was workin' under cover."

"Damn."

Neither of them spoke for a long moment, the sheriff sucking placidly on his peppermint and eyeing Shamrock speculatively.

"This Soholt," Lobell said, "used to be a deputy of mine. That's an old game of his with strangers. He must have seen you—that face, it gives you away."

"That wasn't it."

"No. He come into the office when I was out rustlin' grub for the prisoners. When I come back he was gone, but there was a whole pile of reward posters on the desk that he'd took from the drawer. Yours was on top."

Shamrock studied his face, but his eyes were unseeing.

Would he have to get out, leave without settling with Hyatt? Some stubborn daring in him said no, he'd be damned if he would.

"Did you know that this afternoon?" he asked.

Lobell nodded. "You told me your name, remember? It come to me right off."

"Who else knows it?"

"No one. That's what I'm tryin' to tell you. Why git spooky? I tore the poster up. Ain't nobody seen it or ever will again."

"They better not," Shamrock said softly.

And he turned and left. At the hotel, five doors past the corner and on the same side of the street as the sheriff's office, he asked for a room, paid for it, and got his key.

The room was on the second floor back, and Shamrock opened the door and stood inside a moment, listening. Then he locked the door, walked to the window, pulled the shade, and lighted the lamp.

He did not take his clothes off, but rolled a smoke and lay on the bed. As a matter of practice Shamrock never believed a man's word until he had caught him telling the truth. The sheriff, now, had him guessing. Had Lobell, unarmed and alone out there on the trail, recognized him as a wanted man and tolled him into Malpais Springs on some fake scheme of the moment, so he could send a gunman, this Soholt, over to pick a fight and collect bounty? Or had Lobell told the truth, that he wanted the notice served on Hyatt and was willing to pay for it? If so, then Shamrock knew he was safe for the time being, since Lobell wouldn't collect bounty until Shamrock had finished the job. His natural sense of preservation warned him to get out of a place where reward posters were out for him, but the thought of leaving Hyatt canceled all that.

He stood up, took the lamp over to the washstand, and turned it high. Then he adjusted the mirror, let his hands fall to his sides, and looked at his face a long minute.

"Three times in five days," he said softly.

Then he blew the lamp, opened his door, and looked up and down the corridor. When he was sure no one was coming, he walked to the end of the hall, raised the corridor window, and threw out the rope that served as the fire escape.

In five seconds he was in the alley, walking down it, crossing the street behind the adobe jail which joined the sheriff's office, and down that alley to the livery stable, which he entered by the corrals at the rear. He walked down the centerway until he came to Blue. The lantern was still standing by the door.

Blue nickered a little, and Shamrock's hand stole over his nose. He knew Blue was still thirsty. "Easy, boy," he muttered. "You can't make up for it in a night."

He scratched Blue's ear a moment, then climbed up on the manger, noting passively that his saddle was handy. Then he swung up to the rafter of the hayloft, lifted himself up, and in five minutes was asleep, buried deep in the hay, a gun folded in his hand.

CHAPTER FOUR

THERE IS A QUALITY in a good horse that indefinably sets him apart from the common run. In the cattle country, a good ranch has a little of that quality, too. Shamrock had spent as little time on a ranch as he could help, for there was work and toil and roping and riding, long hours and scant pay for labor in fair weather and foul. It didn't appeal to him. Yet when he topped the ridge across the valley from where the Double Diamond lay, he was quick to see it was no ordinary spread.

It lay high in the foothills of the Santa Ritas, its back to the mountains. The cedar and piñon had given way to sparse timber here, and although the country was broken with small canyons and large mesas, there were vast rolling sweeps of grama-grass range that seemed to stretch endlessly from the Double Diamond front door to the dry country below.

The house itself lay in dark, thick pines, a sprawling log affair with a sloping roof. Along with its outbuildings, it sprawled over a level bench that seemed inserted in the hills. There were two big log barns, a bunkhouse, cookshack, wagon sheds, and a half-dozen pole corrals to the north of the house. There was a rugged dignity about it that advertised at once that it was primarily there for the business of ranching, and ranching on a big scale. Whatever beauty it held had come with time and weather and use, for it fitted into the country with the rugged personality of its surrounding trees and grazing lands.

Shamrock studied it for a long moment, not awed, but curious. Men of Hyatt's stripe usually came from a background of poverty and shiftlessness; but no poverty here, nor, from the looks of the place, any shiftlessness.

The dispossess notice was folded in his hip pocket, forgotten, as he turned down the slope toward the wagon road leading to the place.

As he approached, he saw no one, but the corral gate was wide. Blue was through it before a man stepped out of the bunkhouse and strode over to him.

Shamrock pulled Blue up and waited. The man approaching was middle-aged, his walk slow with authority and with the saddle-stiffness of years. His clothes were worn and clean, but the gun slung at his thigh was ivory-handled, expensive. As he came closer, Shamrock made out his face, squinting a little from habit. It was seamed, half-

THE MAN ON THE BLUE

hidden by a ragged, sandy mustache whose lower fringe was stained with tobacco. The eyes were pale and inquisitive and fearless under the sweep of the worn Stetson. Foreman, Shamrock judged.

Then Shamrock ceased watching him and examined the spread. The house was shaded in front by a huge cottonwood, and there were flowers around it. The logs were huge, scarred dark, the windows deep-set and spacious. The corral lot was clean of litter, and everything seemed neat and sturdy and in order, even to the even rows of brands which were burned into the logs of the bunkhouse.

When his gaze rested again on the man, he was standing beside Blue. Shamrock looked him over coolly.

"I'm lookin' for Hyatt."

The foreman put his thumbs in his belt and spread his booted feet a little in a characteristic gesture of patient parley. He spat deliberately, then turned and looked over the corral lot with the identical, studied arrogance that Shamrock had used. Then he looked at Shamrock.

"I'm his foreman. What can I do for you?"

"Nothin'. I'm lookin' for Hyatt."

The foreman hesitated. "I don't see him, do you?" And he looked around again, with studied pretense.

When his gaze returned to Shamrock, he was staring into the round black hole in the end of a Colt barrel.

"Not yet," Shamrock said.

The foreman's old face did not change as he spat, "That's a purty horse you got."

"All right."

"I'd hate to see him shot out from under you."

Shamrock said nothing, did not take his gaze nor his gun from the man.

"We've been kinda' partic'lar what sort of rider we welcome around here lately—so dang partic'lar we keep a man with a gun at the bunkhouse window."

35

"I'll get you first," Shamrock said evenly. "Where's Hyatt?"

"He won't like your face," the foreman said slowly. "I don't myself."

Shamrock hefted his gun a little, but his face did not change.

"Blow off," he said quietly. "He may like my face better than yours after a pistol-whipping." He eased out of the saddle and jumped lightly to the ground, his Colt beading the foreman as if answering to a magnet.

"Just flip out that gun."

The foreman hesitated only a second, then he did as he was bid, and his gun fell to the ground.

"Now."

"You really want to see him?"

"Now."

The foreman turned and called toward a wagon shed. "Mayo!"

A muffled voice answered, and Shamrock holstered his gun, then kicked the foreman's gun well to the other side of Blue.

"Gent to see you!" the foreman answered.

"Stand off," Shamrock said. The foreman backed off twenty feet, and Shamrock followed him, so as to get Blue out of the line of fire.

Then he turned sideways a little and waited.

"You're a fool," the foreman said softly. "Just a damn fool. He's a gun fighter."

Shamrock said nothing, for at that moment a man stepped out of the wagon shed, hatless, and started walking toward him.

It was the Idaho Hyatt, all right. He was a tall man, yet his leanness was deceiving. His rather blocky head, covered with a curly mat of flaming-red hair, was set low on square shoulders, and his walk was lithe, like that of a man who

36

didn't carry much weight. He was studying Shamrock with green, untroubled eyes. His nose was short, pugnacious as his jaw, and his big deceptive-looking hands swung close to his sides.

Hyatt was halfway to them when he hesitated in his stride, then increased it.

"Ireland!" he said slowly, and laughed deep in his chest. "My God, are you a ghost? I thought you'd be dead."

Shamrock said nothing, only shifted his weight forward onto the balls of his feet.

"Is it—yes, it's you," Hyatt said, still walking.

"I've waited a long time, Hyatt," Shamrock said flatly, "but I generally catch up."

Something in his tone pulled Hyatt up short a dozen yards away. His face changed just a little with the closing of his mouth and the fading of his broad smile.

"Oh. So that's it."

"Any time," Shamrock said softly. "Any time now, you cheap Judas. Any time."

"Wait!" Hyatt commanded sharply. "Wait! You've got it wrong. Let me talk."

Shamrock was folded into himself, and he did not move.

"All you want. Only hurry it up."

"Remember Heffner that was sidin' me up in the Calicos? He got to the sweeper and bought all he wanted to know. He's the one that crossed us. Him and that sweeper sold out to the sheriff Friday noon for your bounty and mine. That night, when I drifted into town from the west, that sweeper trailed me. Right close to the bank, he knifed me in the back, and I got him when all the racket started."

He paused, watching Shamrock, but Shamrock's face was immobile.

"I spent two weeks flat on my face in that hardware store woodshed where I crawled," Hyatt continued grimly. "I heard them take you, but I couldn't move. When I could finally crawl, I'd pull myself out into the alley and crawl down to the garbage heap by the restaurant and eat. I got my water from that horse trough behind the bank."

"Think it over, mister," the foreman said softly. "He never sold a man in his life."

"Does that sound like I crossed you?" Hyatt said. "When I could stand up, I traveled at night. I was so weak it took me three nights to make Joe Manero's. He'd lit a shuck for Nevada. I stayed hid there another week, then stole a horse and left the Territory. By that time you'd broke jail and I tried to get word of you, but you'd gone. I never did hear of you since."

Shamrock's expression did not change. "Where'd they take me to jail, then?"

"Tuscororah County," Hyatt answered promptly. "They was afraid of a lynchin' in Cosmos. You broke jail there a week later."

Shamrock sneered. "You could have picked that up from any stage driver."

Hyatt flushed. "Do you think I'm afraid of you, Ireland?" he asked gently. "Hell, I know you're fast—faster'n me, but I'll fight you, if that's what you want. I'll fight you for your Stetson, but I won't fight you over that. What'll it be?"

"It won't be anything," a voice called from the corner of the ranch house, and without looking up, Shamrock knew it was the girl.

"Ah," the foreman said in a quiet sigh of relief.

The girl was walking toward them, a carbine slacked just off her shoulder. Her eyes were on Shamrock, who had not looked at her once.

"One of Lobell's men?" she asked coldly.

"Call her off," Shamrock said thickly.

"Call me off!" the girl blazed. "If there's any calling done, I'll do it! And I am doing it! Unbuckle that belt and let it fall, then ride out of here!"

"That does it, mister," the foreman said, and he took a step toward Shamrock.

Shamrock moved one step away from the foreman and said, "Huh-uh," but he never took his gaze from Hyatt. The girl waited a long second for him to obey her, then the gun swung up to her shoulder.

"I'll give you three seconds to do it, mister—starting now."

Hyatt yelled, "Nancy! Stop! You're wrong! He's—"

But the girl went ahead counting and when she got to two, Hyatt dived at her.

And as Shamrock tensed at Hyatt's movement, he felt a terrible, explosive blow on his head. He lost consciousness as he started to fall.

CHAPTER FIVE

WHEN SHAMROCK WAKENED, he was staring at a square ceiling. He lay there looking at it, smelling something sweet that seemed to pervade the room. He was undressed and he was in bed; that much he knew. He raised himself on an elbow, looking around him, and immediately something in his head began to roll around like loose shot. He lay down with a groan, but he had seen enough.

This was a girl's room, as the bottled gimcracks on the rough dresser, the flimsy curtains, and the huge mirror testified. But whose? Then he remembered.

So she shot me, he mused. He felt his head. There was a slim bandage circling it, a little thicker behind his left ear.

He sat up with an effort and threw the covers from him, looking for his clothes. Finally, when he had even looked under the bed, he concluded they had taken them. Sitting down on the bed again, he cursed.

A rattle of the doorknob interrupted him, and he dived under the covers as the door swung open and Hyatt, Nancy, and the foreman came in.

He glared hostilely at them.

"Come out of it, huh?" the foreman said, a note of regret in his voice.

Shamrock was watching Hyatt, who came over and sat down on the foot of the bed.

"I'm sorry about that, Ireland. We've got no call to fight."

"Sorry?" Nancy said bitterly. "After that dispossess notice we found in his clothes?"

Shamrock looked at her curiously. Her hair was almost mahogany-colored in the failing light, for evening was coming on. Out of the sun, her freckles were gone, too, and she stood straight as a ramrod, with a quiet arrogance that Shamrock had noticed when he first set eyes on her. She was small, and yet she wasn't—or was it something in her defiant spirit that made Shamrock undecided? He had never known a girl he couldn't buy drinks for, that he couldn't turn away from like a piece of cold food when he was tired of her. But this girl was different, not his kind— or their kind—and he observed her with the same interest with which he might have studied a two-headed calf.

"What about that?" Hyatt asked. "I never heard you hired out your gun to the law."

Shamrock let his gaze leave the girl and yawned.

"I was goin' to throw it away. I forgot," he said coldly.

"Then you weren't workin' for Lobell?"

Shamrock frowned and thought a minute. "Not exactly. He paid me to serve it. I wanted the money, and I wanted to see you. That's all. So I took it."

"You lie!" Nancy said coldly. She turned to Mayo. "He's

a hired gunman of Lobell's—just like all the others are!"

Hyatt turned to her quickly, wrathfully, and she flinched from the anger in his eyes.

"I know him, sis," Hyatt said gently to her. "Let me talk." He turned to Shamrock. "Do you believe that about the Cosmos business?"

"No," Shamrock said promptly.

"All right. Do you remember that day up in the Calicos when you run across me swimmin' in Little Fork?"

Shamrock nodded warily.

"You saw my back. Was there a scar on it?"

Shamrock shook his head. "No."

Hyatt stood up and peeled the shirt off his back and turned so Shamrock could see. The muscles corded and rippled as he moved, smoothed out as he hunched over, and there, just under the right shoulder blade, was a scar raised high with proud flesh.

"The sweeper did it. Do you believe me?"

"Let it go."

"Do you?"

"I reckon."

"You got to," Hyatt said grimly. "I've done a lot of things, Ireland, but I never sold any man out to the law. I'd sooner lose my hand than do it."

Shamrock studied Hyatt's eyes for a full moment, and he decided that Hyatt was telling the truth. "All right. Let it go."

Hyatt stood up, suddenly indifferent and weary.

"Good. You're free to go or do anything you want." He spoke to the foreman. "Matt, get him what he wants."

He turned and left the room, Nancy behind him.

Matt glared at Shamrock. "Well?"

"Clothes."

Matt went out and in a minute returned with Shamrock's clothes and gun. When he had gone, Shamrock got up and dressed. He was so weak he had to sit down twice in the process, but he kept at it stubbornly. His coming had been a blunder, a bad blunder, because he had innocently effected the errand Lobell had sent him on. Hyatt hadn't been killed in the serving of the paper, but he had read the dispossess notice, which was one of Lobell's aims. Shamrock hated that, for he had not intended to meddle in the fight between Lobell and the Hyatts, but there it was—done. He wanted to get out and away.

Dressed, he buckled on his belt after first examining his gun to see if it had been tampered with. His step was a bit unsteady as he opened the door onto a short hall that connected with the main living-room.

It was a large room with a massive fireplace opposite the door. On the walls were game heads and bright Navajo blankets. A huge davenport was pulled up to the fireplace, back to him. On the floor were bear and lion rugs. There was little other furniture—a full gunrack, some chairs—but what there was looked heavy and masculine. It bore the stamp of a man's living.

Shamrock goggled at it a moment, for it had a permanence, an ease, that was strange and hostile to him. Then he made straight for the outside door.

Suddenly he paused, arrested by a strange noise. He listened. It sounded like someone crying. Looking around, his glance settled on the huge davenport, for the sound was coming from there.

He hesitated, then walked slowly over to it.

There, huddled up against a pile of pillows, Nancy Hyatt lay sobbing as if her heart would break.

Shamrock watched a moment, his face immobile. Then he cleared his throat. The girl whirled at the sound and tried to stifle her sobs. Shamrock saw the bitterness and hostility creep into her eyes like some dark pain.

"I'm lookin' for my horse," Shamrock said.

"Did you expect to find him here?"

"No. Where is he?"

"In the corral, of course. Did you think we'd steal him?"

"No," he said doggedly. "I'm leavin'."

He looked at her curiously, studying the fine, soft features that he had never seen look gentle.

"If you expect me to apologize for shooting you, I won't," Nancy said bluntly. "I wish I'd been a better shot."

Shamrock nodded. He understood that kind of talk. "I don't."

"I—I don't suppose it's courtesy to insult a guest in your own house, either," she continued bitterly, "but I don't like meddling fools—fools who blunder other people into trouble along with themselves!"

"I don't, either," Shamrock said coldly. "It might teach you to stay out of a man's pockets."

The girl jumped up, her eyes blazing. "Get out of here! You cheap, cold-faced gunman. The next time I get a gun in my hands, I won't miss!"

"Save it. I'm leavin'," Shamrock said, then added softly, "You she-gunman."

The girl made a lunge for the gunrack, but Shamrock was ahead of her. He stood in front of it while she clawed frantically at the guns. He held her off at arm's length, watching her with a kind of curious alertness. At last she stopped struggling. Shamrock, without turning around, took each gun down from the rack and ejected it empty of shells. She watched him do it, and when he was finished, she drew back her hand and slapped his face. He made no move to dodge, even though he saw it coming.

"That's twice," Shamrock said. "You little killer."

"You lie!" she cried. "You lie, you lie!"

"Once on me, once on Lobell," Shamrock reminded her calmly. "I'm a gunman, but I never hid behind a skirt."

"Do you call it killing when you try to save your brother

from being murdered?"

"Maybe I was aiming to fight him," Shamrock conceded, "but you didn't know that. You—"

"I don't know anything about your past quarrels with Mayo!" she flared. "But I know you were sent out here by Lobell to kill him! And I know I'd kill you and Lobell cheerfully, and hang for it!"

"Isn't there a man on the place that will fight?" Shamrock jeered. "Or do you like it so well they let you?"

"Oh, you fool! You poor, blind fool. Have they hired you to kill and not told you that you can't lose—that Mayo can't win?"

"He's a gunman."

"And the minute he draws a gun on a man that's got the nerve to come out and face him like you did today, the whole slope will be up in arms against him! Don't you know that he's paroled on good behavior—that a gun fight means prison, or worse?"

She paused, her breast heaving with anger.

"Why do you think I tried to drag that snake of a Lobell? Do you think I want to die? It's to save Mayo from killing him, and getting killed by a lynch mob himself! Mayo's going straight! He's going straight if I have to die to give him a chance! And he's going straight on the Double Diamond—his father's place, the place that they've stolen from him!"

Her voice choked up suddenly and she turned from him. "Get out! What do you know about love—about love for a brother, or for the place you were born? You're a gun-crazy killer—like the man that pays you. Get out!"

"I'll go," he said.

He stepped around her and walked toward the door.

"Wait," she said.

When he stopped and turned, he saw her chin was quivering, but her head was up, proud.

"Would it hurt you to do a favor for me—a favor that won't harm you—or Lobell?"

"What is it?"

"Don't—don't mention to Mayo that I tried to kill Lobell. Don't ever let him know it. Can't—can't you see what it would mean—what he would do?"

"I won't," Shamrock said, and walked out.

Outside, he leaned against the doorjamb a moment to take some of the weight off his shaking knees. A few minutes ago, he hadn't given a thought to the sheriff's quarrel with the Hyatts, but now he thought he understood it—part of it, that is. Hyatt was paroled, and to defy the law with a gun meant prison, yet in his belief that the Double Diamond had been stolen from him, he dared to defend it with guns. His warning had been given, and Lobell had heeded it up till now. Then Shamrock came along, a gunman, by his looks, and a good one. Lobell hired him to serve the paper and thereby complete all the requirements of the law. He had done it in a fumbling, accidental way that was no less effective in its results. Meanwhile, Nancy had been willing to give her life to get Lobell out of the way, and remove his threat to her brother and the Double Diamond. A foolish, fantastic scheme, but it had a pathos that Shamrock did not miss, and could scarcely understand. Why Lobell? Was he any more than a blundering, crooked sheriff that took office because he was too lazy to ranch?

He could see Blue off in the horse corral. The sun already was so low the valley was in shadow, and the old lone cottonwood in front of the house had stopped the daylong rustling of its leaves as the quiet of evening came on. Far off he could hear the measured bawling trumpet of a cow calling her early calf. Closer, from the barns, he could hear the thin chitter of swallows. To him it seemed suddenly peaceful and right. Worth fighting for, hadn't she said?

I'm gettin' soft, he mused, as he straightened up and headed for the corral. He tried to think of where he should go after Blue was saddled. The mountains, all right, but where? And where after that?

Blue walked up to the bars and nickered as he approached, and Shamrock scratched his ears. The cheery sound of banging pans came from the cookshack, and a glance over his shoulder told Shamrock the hands were washing up. Their horses were in the corral watching him with curious but trustful eyes.

He rolled a cigarette and lighted it, and Blue backed away out of the smoke, watching him reproachfully. Shamrock knew he should get Blue saddled and be off, but he felt a reluctance to leave that was hard to define.

Blue flicked his ears just a little when Shamrock sighed, dragged his foot off the corral bar, and dropped his cigarette. He headed for the bunkhouse.

On the way to it, he had to pass the wagon shed, and Matt stepped out beside him.

"Where's Hyatt?" Shamrock asked.

The foreman did not answer, simply looked at Shamrock.

"It's not that," Shamrock said. "I want to talk to him."

"He's down at the far barn."

Shamrock walked steadily across the corral lot to the barn. Hyatt was just closing the big door when he saw Shamrock. He finished his job, then came over.

"Better stay for supper."

"Is this straight about Lobell?" Shamrock asked bluntly.

"Has Nancy been talkin' to you?"

Shamrock nodded.

"Yes," Hyatt said.

"You can't go down and choose him because you're on parole. Is that it?"

Hyatt nodded.

"But why Lobell? He's only the law. You've lost the spread to the bank."

"Have we?" Hyatt said quietly. "Lobell was a horse trader before he was sheriff. He got the office because the ranchers in this country are too damned selfish—too busy makin' money on beef—to put up a good man or run themselves. Lobell's stopped all the rustlin' in the county—except the Double Diamond stuff. And he won't try to stop that. He's sat by and seen us rustled into debt, to ruin, and all the ranchers of the Santa Rita slope have stood by and watched it, too."

"Why?"

"Because they hated my dad. Dad was a hard man, and a successful one. He got the best land and most of the water in the country by shrewd bargainin'. They hate me because I ran off with the Wild Bunch and turned against Dad. And they hate me more since I got home. They're afraid of me, and they're glad the Double Diamond is lost. If I went to town and combed the sheriff out, even drew a gun on him, they'd be here with a lynch mob in an hour."

"But Lobell don't get the spread."

"No," Hyatt said bitterly. "It's the bank. Dad borrowed money up to his neck to get more land and stock. After he was killed—a miner gulched him one night—they started clampin' down. Our paper had time to run, but they called it in. I wasn't here. Matt was shorthanded. Nancy was tryin' to run the place. They saw a chance to get the ranch and they took it. We haven't even got a corral count of beef left. The range is cleaned. The place is in their hands—almost. It's up to Lobell to evict us, and he'll do it for the pleasure."

"What can you do?"

"Fight."

"What good'll that do?"

Hyatt looked off over the hills before he answered, and when he did his voice was husky with passion. "Only this. I'll kill Lobell if I can and I'll down a dozen of these pious ranchers—neighbors. I'll get troops here before they get me out. They'll remember the Hyatts and the Double Diamond as long as men talk in this country. And Lobell will only be a memory along with us."

"What do you figure he aims to do now?"

"He'll come out and warn us to get off. I'll run him off the place. Then he'll be out with a posse." He spread his hands expressively. "Then we'll fight to the finish."

Shamrock hitched up his belt. "I see," he said softly. "And I brought it on—the showdown."

"It had to come," Hyatt said grimly. "Lobell's playin' it legal, so we can't resort to law. He's been tryin' to serve that paper for a month, and nobody would do it till you come along. Now it's served. We're ready."

"I've got three thousand on my head in this Territory," Shamrock said slowly. "It wouldn't help much if I was to side with you, would it?"

"That would give him one more excuse for saltin' us down."

"It's hard lines," Shamrock said.

"Thanks, anyway."

Shamrock started to walk away, then paused. "If it looks like I'm buyin' in this fight, don't get me wrong, will you?"

Hyatt frowned, puzzled.

"Just remember that. Don't get me wrong."

And before Hyatt had a chance to answer, Shamrock walked over to the corral.

As he was saddling Blue he knew what he should do. There was three thousand dollars on his head, and to a man of Shamrock's experience that meant only one thing. Lobell, now that the paper was served and Shamrock was useless to him, would start bounty-hunting. All the traveled trails leading out of the country would be guarded. He was the prey of the first man who could ambush him. The thing to do, then, was to hit for the mountains and ride out of the country.

So when he left the Double Diamond, he headed for the hill west of the place toward the mountains.

Once over the hump out of sight of the spread, however, he changed his course and started a long circle of the ranch. In twenty minutes, he was on the road heading for Malpais Springs, a cool night wind in his face.

I think I like this job bein' a deputy, he said to himself. *Yes, sir. I think I'll stay.*

For Shamrock was hard to convince. Lobell had paid him a thousand dollars to kill Hyatt or serve the paper, preferably both. That was a lot of cash for a man to put out for the satisfaction of seeing a spread ruined. It was more than spite, as Hyatt believed. Nancy sensed something, Shamrock knew, but she had not mentioned it. This morning, when Lobell had paid him the first five hundred, he hadn't thought much about it. Now he was curious, and cynical. He thought again of Nancy's willingness to die for her brother, and for his chance to go straight.

They ain't my kind of folks, Shamrock reflected as he pulled Blue off the road and headed for Malpais Springs. *I reckon they're a heap better, too.*

The sun was fading out of the flatlands below when he said aloud, "Yes, sir. I think I'll buy into this."

CHAPTER SIX

WHEN SHAMROCK looped Blue's reins over the hitchrack in front of the sheriff's office, then turned and looked at the lighted window, there was a quiet gleam of amusement in his eyes. It died as he crossed the sidewalk. He would be about as welcome to the sheriff here in town as an epidemic of Texas fever, and he didn't doubt Lobell would use the same measures to rid himself of both.

A man was seated at the sheriff's roll-top desk as Shamrock opened the door. He had his feet cocked up, and was deep in a saddle catalogue. Except for a pair of predatory black eyes, the man looked like the usual puncher—range clothes, no shave, battered Stetson, worn six-gun. Shamrock saw the badge on his vest, felt the surly air of petty authority about him, and guessed the man was the jailer whom he had not seen that morning when Lobell gave him the papers.

"A man gen'rally knocks when he comes in here," the jailer said heavily.

"That's fine," Shamrock said amiably, looking around him. "What does he do when he goes out?"

The jailer scowled darkly and laid down his catalogue. Shamrock cuffed the Stetson off his forehead and put his hands on his hips.

"What do *you* want?"

"That's better," Shamrock said pleasantly. "Where's Lobell?"

"He ain't in."

"I can see that. Where is he?"

"Anything you got to say to him, you can say to me," the man said importantly.

"I reckon I could, but I won't."

The jailer heaved his feet off the desk and swiveled his chair to face Shamrock.

"Cocky, isn't he?" he sneered.

"No. Just patient," Shamrock said softly, and something in his voice made the jailer's eyes alert. "I asked you where Lobell was. I heard you say he was out. Where?"

The jailer suddenly sat upright in his chair. "Say, you ain't—you couldn't be—"

"The new deputy," Shamrock said.

The jailer's mouth slacked open a little, then he closed it and jumped out of the chair. He laughed uncomfortably. "Well, now—I—uh—" He rubbed his open palm on his pants leg with an uneasy motion. "I didn't think you'd—uh—be back." He paused, then added hastily, "So soon." Shamrock watched him narrowly, his expression unchanging.

"My name's Coyne—Ed Coyne."

Still Shamrock said nothing.

"Yours is Ire—" The man stopped talking, bogged down, then tried a quick recovery. "Ireland, I heard that danged Soholt say last night."

"Let it go," Shamrock said coldly. He walked over to the desk, took the man's chair, and sat down in it and leaned back.

"I reckon I better—"

"Where's Lobell?" Shamrock cut in.

"I don't know, and that's a fact," Coyne said earnestly. "He just left a little before supper and never said where to nor how long he'd be gone."

Nor who he was hunting, Shamrock thought grimly. He looked around the room at the windows. The office was on a corner, a window on each street side; but the desk was behind the door in the corner, so that a man sitting behind it could not be seen from the street. There were a dozen fly-specked reward posters tacked up on the plank walls whose whitewash had long since peeled off. In the west wall, a steel door led into the 'dobe-walled jail. A made-up cot near it, three straight armchairs, two spittoons, and a loaded gunrack made up the rest of the furniture.

"I reckon I'll step out a minute," the jailer said after a few seconds' wait. "I'm out of the makin's."

51

Shamrock said carelessly, "You better stay." He flipped his Durham sack to the jailer, then picked up the deck of cards that had been lying on the desk. He shuffled them carelessly, while the jailer backed up to one of the wall chairs and sat down. His hands were trembling so that he made three attempts to build a smoke before he succeeded. Shamrock pretended not to notice.

His game was solitaire, and for two hours he dealt it, the jailer watching in utter quiet. Shamrock did not even look at him again. Only once did he move, and that was to get up and open the door a few inches with the comment, "It's hot."

He didn't know how much time had passed when he heard the sound of several horses being ridden up to the rack.

The jailer made a motion to get up, but Shamrock looked up from his cards and the man sat down again, squirming with unease.

The jumble of voices and the creak of saddle leather were all Shamrock could hear, then the talk suddenly stopped.

"Well, I'll be damned!" a voice said. "Ain't that his blue?"

The boardwalk thumped, then Shamrock heard a low, exclamatory whistle.

"No wonder—"

"Cut it!" a voice cut in softly. It was Lobell's.

There was a whispered conference which Shamrock did not hear, then he heard footsteps and the door opened.

Lobell was alone. His face was composed, benevolent, and he looked mildly and pleasantly surprised when he saw Shamrock.

"Well, well," he said with gruff good humor. "Back, huh?"

Shamrock nodded, his face still. The sheriff turned to

Coyne and jerked his head. Coyne made a quick, hurried exit, and the sheriff shut the door after him. Shamrock kept his seat, and the sheriff walked over to the desk and threw a leg over the corner of it and rubbed his hands together with a brisk, warming motion.

"It's a mite chill out tonight," he observed pleasantly, studying Shamrock's face with wary, blank eyes. "I went out to look for you," he announced suddenly.

Shamrock tilted the chair back. "I cut corners. I was in a hurry."

"What happened?"

"He took it."

"Did he—uh—fight?"

"A little," Shamrock said. He turned his head so the sheriff could see the raw furrow behind his ear. He had removed the bandage on the way in.

"Ah-h," Lobell said softly. "Is he dead?"

"I had to blow his gun out of his hand," Shamrock lied idly.

Shamrock saw some of the light go out of the sheriff's eyes, but the muscles in his face were perfectly controlled. He leaned back and exhaled his breath. "Good. No bloodshed. That's fine. Everything legal, and in order. Hyatt will live to thank you, son."

"About that other five hundred," Shamrock said coldly.

"That's right," Lobell said cheerfully. He stood up and reached in his hip pocket and drew a wallet from it. He counted out a pile of double eagles on the desk, and Shamrock picked them up and rammed them in his pocket.

"That makes it quits, don't it?"

"I dunno," Shamrock said, looking Lobell straight in the eye. "I sorta like the job."

Lobell said nothing for a moment, his face perfectly still, watching Shamrock, then he laughed. "Sure. It's a good job, and you done it well, son." He reached in his vest for a peppermint drop and slipped it in his mouth, watching Shamrock.

"No. I mean the deputy's job."

"Oh." Lobell's thick hands had ceased fumbling at his wallet and now he was frankly staring at Shamrock. "I'm afraid I can't use you," he said slowly.

"Think a minute," Shamrock said.

"I've thought."

"Think some more, then."

Lobell put the wallet in his pocket and leaned both hands on the desk. "Listen, son, I'd like to. I'd sure like to keep you. You're a good man to work with—but it can't be done. You're a wanted man. Could I hire a deputy that's got a pitcher in every sheriff's office in the whole Territory —in all the Territories?"

"The only man that knows that is dead—besides us," Shamrock said. "Just us two," he jibed softly.

"Men travel," Lobell said evasively. "What if some puncher from Sahuaro County that has seen your description in the sheriff's office rode into Malpais Springs? How would it look for me?"

"You never saw the poster. It never came."

"Why do you want to stay here?" Lobell asked bluntly, disarmingly. "It's nothin' but a slow cow town, son."

"I like 'em. I'd like to settle down."

"Huh-uh," the sheriff contradicted.

"All right, then. I like the people."

The sheriff said nothing, but his eyes called Shamrock a liar.

"I think I'll stay," Shamrock said again, looking at Lobell. "Out in the fresh air, not much excitement, and it pays good money," he jeered.

"Not any more."

"All right. What pay does a deputy get?"

"Fifty a month and horse keep."

"That's fine. You've got yourself a deputy."

Suddenly the sheriff laughed, all good humor again. "Son, you're stubborn. I don't need another deputy, but danged if I don't need a man as stubborn as you are. You're hired."

"I know it," Shamrock answered.

The sheriff was smiling now. "You've got a job. You just take this here badge"—he drew a deputy's badge from a drawer—"and tote it anywhere, inside your pocket if you want. Then go down and tell McKinley to put your horse keep on the county account."

"Who?" Shamrock asked, rising from the chair, making sure that he could not be seen from the street.

"McKinley, that kid at the stables."

"You mean Maginnis."

"McKinley, his name is."

"All right," Shamrock said. "McKinley, then. That tow-headed kid."

Lobell was rolling a smoke and he suddenly stopped. "What did you call him?"

"Maginnis."

"That's funny," Lobell said, his face still, watchful, his hands poised. "Where'd you hear that name?"

"He calls himself that," Shamrock said, puzzled.

"He said so?"

"He said so."

Lobell dropped the makings, spun around on his heel, and swung the door open.

"Come in here!" he called flatly.

Three men, one of them Coyne, shuffled into the room. Another was a blond man with the palest skin and hair Shamrock had ever seen on a man. He was fastidiously clean, but his clothes were not foppish. The third was swart, squat, thick, with cunning black eyes. Gunmen, both of them. Lobell ignored them.

"I hope you're right," he said slowly, looking at Shamrock. "Are you sure?"

"What? His name's Maginnis? I only got his word for it."

"Bueno," the sheriff said, a broad smile on his face. "Son, you bring me luck." He slid a look over at the three men waiting for orders, then explained. "That kid Maginnis is a killer. He's the ranahan that knocked over the Cattleman's Trust in Lobato Wells two months ago and killed the cashier." He turned to the three men. "You remember it?"

It seemed to Shamrock that their nods were uncertain.

"I should have knowed it," the sheriff said. "Dang me, but I should. Come to think of it, he fits the description to a hair. But he's only a kid." He looked shrewdly at Shamrock. "Nothing but a kid." He shook his head gravely. "But you can't tell. Seems like nowadays they go bad younger." He sighed regretfully. "I hate to do it, but we'd best take him in. And we got to be careful, because he's salty."

He pointed to Coyne. "Ed, you come with me and Ireland. We'll go to the stables by the corral door. Pace"—he pointed to the blond man—"you and Freed go up to the front. One of you stand just inside the door, the other get by the side of the building in case he goes through a window."

"Wait a minute," Shamrock cut in. "Are we thinkin' of the same kid?"

"Sure. Gangly, light hair, innocent eyes, and sort of nice ways?"

"He ain't a killer," Shamrock said flatly.

"That's what I say. They go bad young," the sheriff said piously. "Well, we'll git him and send him over to Sahuaro County. That's all we can do." He motioned the three men out, then waited for Shamrock. At a sign from Shamrock, Lobell stepped out onto the walk and Shamrock followed him.

"You got it, Pace?" Lobell asked.

"I got it."

Shamrock glanced over at the hitchrack. Besides Blue, there were five horses at the rack. That meant there were two more men who had ridden in with the sheriff to account for. Shamrock looked fleetingly at the sheriff as they turned down the side street, but Lobell's face was grave and serious. Coyne dropped in beside Shamrock.

At the alley, they turned in, and together walked down it. It was dark, so Shamrock fell back a step and let his hands hang loose, ready.

A little way from the stables, the sheriff halted them. "We're takin' no chances," he whispered. "We'll go in the back. Coyne, you travel close to the stalls on the far side. Me, I'll take the near side. Ireland, you take the middle. If Pace or Freed spook him, he'll high-tail it down the centerway and out the back."

"He'll be in bed," Shamrock said.

"Take no chances," the sheriff repeated. "It'll be dark, so watch it."

The stable had a wide aisle running the length of it, a huge front and back entrance, wide and high enough to accommodate a load of hay. It was down this that they intended to go, working up toward the office.

Looking in the back door, the far front entrance was made easily distinguishable by the light of the town. As they stepped inside, Shamrock said, "Listen. No gunplay. That kid's all right. Talk to him all you want, but no gunplay."

"That's right," the sheriff seconded. "No bloodshed. Now spread out." He paused, then said distinctly, "Now remember, I'm on the left facin' front, Coyne is on the right, Ireland, you're in the middle."

They fanned out to their positions, leaving Shamrock standing alone. He stood there listening, as the footfalls of

Coyne and the sheriff grew dimmer.

Shamrock drew his gun. A whisper from the sheriff reached him.

"You there, Ireland?"

Shamrock walked swiftly ahead, then answered, "Yes."

He paused and looked behind him. It was a well of blackness to the rear and to both sides, but he realized that he would be perfectly silhouetted against the light of the front entrance to anyone behind him.

Far ahead on the street, he saw a shadowy figure step through the big door and lose himself in the darkness of the stalls. That would be Pace.

Shamrock paused and listened. He could not fight the crawling feeling out of his back. He was sure now that Lobell had arrived at the office with four men. The sheriff had seen Shamrock's horse, knew that Blue would be put up in the stable, and had sent two men ahead to hide in the stable for Shamrock and for their bounty. Were they behind him?

Maybe they had a bead on him now, but Shamrock resolved to move anyway. He dropped quietly on all fours, and moved swiftly to the right, toward Coyne's side. Once close to the stalls, he rose and listened.

Coyne was ahead of him. Softly Shamrock padded up behind him. He touched Coyne's clothing in the dark and he felt Coyne jerk away. Swiftly he rammed his Colt into flesh.

"Not a sound," he warned softly. Coyne stopped, and Shamrock could hear his quick breathing. With a deft movement of his free hand, Shamrock had Coyne's gun in his own belt.

He leaned close to Coyne. "Walk out in the middle," he ordered.

Coyne did not move, and Shamrock jabbed hard with his gun. Slowly, reluctantly, the jailer moved out toward the middle of the centerway. Shamrock could hear his frightened breathing.

If there were men behind them now, they could see both Shamrock and Coyne silhouetted. If they were hidden in front, they could see nothing, could only go by Lobell's loudly announced instructions.

Shamrock gathered himself to act when Lobell's voice came out of the dark.

"Ireland?" he said firmly.

Shamrock rammed Coyne ahead, followed close behind him. Then Lobell, for the second time and louder, said, "Ireland!"

Shamrock reached his gun out to one side of Coyne and fired it.

Even in the act, he fell on his face and rolled backward, leaving Coyne fair in the centerway as the whole stable thundered with the concert of gunfire.

He heard a scream, but he kept rolling until he was brought up abruptly against something, then he rose to his knees.

Lobell's position was marked with a twin pencil of orange. A little beyond him on the opposite side of the stables by Blue's stall four guns roared their staccato flashes into the night—the guns of the missing two who were to wait for Shamrock. Pace, too, near the door, was shooting.

Then it died.

Shamrock, a cold smile on his face in the dark, rose and walked slowly forward, keeping to the stalls.

"Bring a light!" Lobell ordered. "Freed, go in there and get that Maginnis kid. The rest of you wait!"

It was Pace up front that struck the match and found the lantern in its usual place by the door, handy for customers. He lighted it and walked back.

Two men stepped out from the stalls to join him, one a slow, rangy man, the other undersize and quick. They all walked toward the body lying in the centerway, a fast growing pool of blood mushrooming out beneath it.

Lobell saw it first, and he stopped.

"God! It's Coyne!"

Quickly he looked up to where Coyne should have been.

There, Shamrock stood leaning against a stall partition, his arms folded, gun in hand, a cold, hard smile on his face, his eyes mocking.

He was the only one with a loaded gun, so he stood utterly still and waited, watching Lobell's face flush out into calmness. For five full seconds Shamrock and the sheriff watched each other.

"I thought Maginnis had made a break for it," Lobell said cautiously.

"So did I," Shamrock said. Lazily, his gun hanging at his side, he walked over to Coyne and prodded the body with his foot. Then he looked up at Lobell.

"What did Coyne shoot at?"

Coyne's empty holster showed plainly before them all, yet not a man had the courage to look at Shamrock—except Lobell.

He looked, and his eyes were smeared over with a fury that he could not control.

"That's too bad," he said, looking at Shamrock. "He was a good man."

"Was he?" Shamrock asked, his voice edged with mockery. "Pity he never had brains, isn't it?"

Lobell nodded briefly and holstered his gun, and only then did Shamrock notice that his breath had been held. Lobell calmly and carelessly reached into his vest pocket and slipped a peppermint in his mouth, placid again.

CHAPTER SEVEN

SHAMROCK WAITED until Maginnis was prodded out of the office. The youngster had dressed hurriedly; his hair was awry, but his eyes, even though the shots had awakened him from a sound sleep, were wide with excitement. And wide with something else, too, Shamrock saw. It was fear.

When Freed, the swart, poker-faced man of little speech, shoved Maginnis into the circle of lantern light, the boy looked first at the sheriff, then at each of the others.

"Maginnis, huh?" the sheriff drawled quietly. "So that's your name?"

The youngster flushed and looked immediately at Shamrock.

"You told him!"

Shamrock nodded.

"So you thought you'd change your name and hide right under the law's nose?" Lobell said sadly. "You got all the makin's of a real bad man, boy."

"What are you goin' to do with me?" Maginnis asked defiantly.

"Do with you? Why, not a thing, sonny. The law over in Sahuaro County will tend to that. And I reckon they'll do to you what they do to all the killers they catch."

"Killers?" Maginnis cried. "I'm not a killer. What have I done?"

Lobell turned to Shamrock and shrugged. "What can I do?" he asked resignedly.

"They claim you stuck up a bank in Lobato Wells and killed the cashier," Shamrock said.

"It's a lie!" Maginnis cried furiously.

"All you got to do is go over with us and prove you never," Lobell said in a kindly voice.

"And stay in jail?" Maginnis asked. His voice went shrill with excitement.

"I reckon."

"I won't!" Maginnis cried. "You murderin' old wolf!" He looked at Shamrock pleadingly. "That's the way he got my—"

But before he could finish the sentence, Freed had raised his gun in a vicious arc and clubbed him with the barrel. The youngster folded up like a rag doll and sprawled on the stable floor. Shamrock cursed, his hand dropping to his gun, but Lobell leaped for Freed and drove a big fist in his face. It sent Freed in a sprawling lunge against a stall partition.

"Damned bully!" Lobell growled savagely. He looked around at his men. "I told you not to hurt that kid."

Shamrock let his gun settle back in its holster, cursing himself because he hadn't been watching Freed when Maginnis was talking. Now the kid was quieted, and Lobell was making another fast recovery. He half turned to Shamrock now.

"Goddlemighty. Can't I get a thing done without gunplay?" he growled, then he cursed them. "Look at Ireland. Not a shot tonight. You act like a bunch of hardcases, the whole lot of you."

He glared at them in stern wrath, and the lot of them looked like whipped dogs. Shamrock's still alert face watched the little play without any expression, but inside he was raging.

Freed got to his feet, holding his jaw. Lobell strode over, yanked him by his shirt collar, then turned him around and kicked him in the rear, kiting him off across the centerway.

Shamrock knelt by Maginnis and felt his head. What had

the kid been about to say when the quick thinking of Freed had silenced him? Maginnis's scalp was bloody, and a welt was slowly rising, but Shamrock doubted if his skull had been fractured.

"How is he?" the sheriff asked gently.

"All right."

"Two of you pick him up and take him over to the jail," Lobell ordered. "And be careful with him. Then come back and get Coyne."

While they were picking Maginnis up, the sheriff knelt by Coyne and turned him over. A heavy bunch of keys dangled from his belt, and Lobell removed them. Shamrock, watching him, noted that Coyne was literally riddled with bullets—slugs meant for himself, he knew. Lobell handled the body gently, reverently, then looked fleetingly at Shamrock and away.

At the jail, the steel door was unlocked and they entered the cell corridor. Two other prisoners—drunks, by their sodden inquisitiveness—watched them put Maginnis in the cell on a cot, then go out. There, Shamrock knew, he was safe for a time.

"Pace, you take over tonight," Lobell instructed. "Here's the keys." He handed them to Pace, then turned to the two gunmen who had been hidden in the stall. "George, you and Harmer go get Coyne and take him over to the hardware store. Freed, stable all them horses." He turned to Shamrock. "I'd like a drink."

Shamrock, as he stepped out the door behind Lobell, thought grimly that he at last had the sheriff's measure. He could understand now the hatred in Nancy's voice as she spoke of Lobell. The sheriff's intentions now were obvious. His attempt with his gunmen to kill Shamrock had failed. He had finally recognized that Shamrock was an easier man to string along with than he was to kill, and with that bland good humor which fooled nobody, least of all Shamrock, he was ready to do an about face and accept Shamrock for the time being as inevitable.

Crossing the street to the Legal Tender, Shamrock anticipated the sheriff's conversation. It could only be about Hyatt, and Shamrock knew that none of his evasion in answering the sheriff's questions would save Hyatt. It could delay things a bit, but then Hyatt said he was ready. So be it.

The crowd at the Legal Tender was thinned out, and the two of them chose a corner away from the few men at the bar. Both ordered small beers.

"What did Hyatt say?" Lobell asked, without any preliminaries.

Shamrock raised his glass thoughtfully, then set it down again.

"Lots of things. Tallied up, he says if you want him off, throw him off."

"Ah," Lobell said softly. "He did, huh? Throw him off. Well, sir, we can do that, too." His eyes were pleased as he asked suddenly, "Do you think he meant it?"

"You better see for yourself."

Lobell chuckled. "I aim to—with about twenty men."

Shamrock looked mildly surprised. "Twenty? Why that many?"

"He'll fight. We'll need that many to get the place."

"Oh," Shamrock said slowly. "I didn't think it was the place you wanted."

"Why'd you think I sent you out there?"

Shamrock looked levelly at him. "I know damned well why you sent me out there. So do you. But that job will cost you more than a thousand."

"I can do it with a posse," Lobell said easily. "Do it easy. Legal, in front of witnesses and in the light of day."

Shamrock reached in his money belt and laid a handful of double eagles on the counter.

"Here's a thousand says you can't."

Lobell did not move for a moment, then he said, "Why not?"

"He won't fight."

"You don't know him."

"I know he's not a fool," Shamrock said. "You show up with twenty men and he'll give up and ride off. Then where'll you be? The posse will get a good laugh out of that."

Twin wrinkles appeared between the sheriff's eyebrows, but he studied his beer placidly. "So he won't fight, huh?" he said softly. "What have I got to do to make him?"

Shamrock thought a moment, although he had the answer ready. Finally he said, "Say you take four or five good men—good men, I mean, and ride out to the Double Diamond. He may talk with you." He looked obliquely at Lobell. "The talk is bound to get tough. If a fight starts, Hyatt is pretty sure to get killed, isn't he? No witnesses except your own. Savvy?"

"Yeah. I think I do," the sheriff said quietly without looking at him. Then he added quietly in a low voice, "Listen, hardcase. What's your play?"

Here it was. Shamrock knew Lobell was watching him in the mirror and he grinned faintly.

"I got a good nose for dinero," he answered softly, and looked up at Lobell's reflection in the mirror. They studied each other, unblinking.

"Take my tip. Light a shuck," the sheriff drawled.

"Take mine, and go to hell."

They looked steadily at each other a moment longer. Suddenly the sheriff chuckled. "What would I do without you?" he asked softly, sweetly sardonic.

"Blunder into a jam," Shamrock answered arrogantly.

The sheriff laughed again, and this time he looked full at Shamrock. "Danged if I don't believe I would. You got a head."

Shamrock said nothing.

Lobell dreamily studied his beer. "Take five-six good men out. He gets proddy. We fight. Maybe some of us get tagged, but he goes down. It's risky."

"You afraid of him?"

"Hell, yes, I am," Lobell answered promptly. "Why do you think I paid you to serve that paper?"

"I'll go out with you."

The sheriff lounged off the bar, laid a dollar on it, and surveyed the room, his face grave and benevolent again. Then he reached into his vest pocket, drew out a peppermint, and put it in his mouth as he turned again to Shamrock.

"Maybe you're right. Come around in the mornin'."

He turned and walked majestically out of the saloon. Behind him, Shamrock was quietly smiling. Each of them had tipped his hand a little; Lobell enough to warn Shamrock to stay out of his game; Shamrock enough to let Lobell think it was money he was after. Shamrock had done him three favors already by serving the paper, uncovering Maginnis, and mapping out a new way to kill Hyatt, and he guessed Lobell wouldn't try to dispose of him as long as he was useful.

And that being so, Shamrock decided to settle another matter. But he wasn't taking chances. He drifted back through the poker tables, past the gaming tables, and out the back door. Then he traveled the alley on the edge of the creek bank a block, came out to the street, and, seeing no one, made his way across the street and back to the hotel.

Again he got his key from the night clerk. Again he went upstairs to his room. But he did not go in. This time he went straight to the corridor window and looked out. He could see nothing, but still he took no chances. Following the L in the corridor to its end, he threw down the rope fire escape and was soon in the alley.

This time he traveled the alley in the same direction. Where it crossed the street behind the jail he waited a moment, keeping in the shadow of some outbuildings while he studied the street. A light burned in the sheriff's office, but not in the jail.

He crossed the street swiftly to the shadow of the jail, waited, then moved to the other side of the alley. There, deep in shadow, he studied the end of the 'dobe jail building. Maginnis was in there in the end cell and with him was something that Shamrock would have given much to know. What the kid had been about to say concerning Lobell that Freed had so expertly cut short might mean something and it might not, but he wanted to know.

Save for the single small window in the end, the jail was windowless. And the lone window was high, perhaps eight feet from the ground.

The chances were that Maginnis was asleep after the bat on the head he had received. If Shamrock called up to him, it would wake the whole jail. It wasn't that the prisoners would call Pace, but what they might overhear that could easily be used to buy them lenience from the sheriff.

He'd have to do better than that. He walked down the alley a way. Behind one of the stores, he saw a barrel set under the eavespout. It was empty, for the spring rains were over. Shamrock picked it up and brought it back to the jail wall and set it under Maginnis's window. Then softly he climbed up on the barrel and straightened up. The window was open and he could just see into the cell corridor, through the bars and the tight mesh screen.

"Maginnis," he called softly. He waited for an answer, and got only a chorus of snores in reply. He called again, and got no reply.

He hesitated a moment, considering that the other two prisoners had obviously been drunks. Nothing short of a commotion would wake them.

He reached in his pants and got a handful of matches. Holding one poised in his hand, he listened to hear if the street was clear. Then he struck the match and rammed it through the wire. It flared, lighting up the jail. Patiently, he went through the handful. When he was finished, he called, "Maginnis!"

This time, a sleepy voice whispered, "Yeah?"

"Maginnis? This is Ireland."

"Who?"

"Is anybody else awake?"

A pause. "I don't think so. Who is it?"

"The man with the blue."

There was a long pause, then Maginnis growled, "What do you want?"

"Can you hear?"

"I don't want to," the youngster retorted.

"I'm tryin' to help you, kid," Shamrock said earnestly.

"Sure," Maginnis sneered. "You helped me a lot."

"What does Lobell want with you? Tell it straight."

"Get out!"

"You little jughead!" Shamrock growled. "I'm tryin' to help you. Can't you see that?"

"Get out!" Maginnis repeated.

"Talk sense," Shamrock pleaded. "I can—"

"*Get the hell out!*" Maginnis yelled loudly.

Shamrock cursed. Even as he did so, he could hear the cell door clang.

"Kid, keep your mouth shut! *Keep it shut!*" Shamrock whispered savagely.

He dodged down below the sill as the cell door swung open.

"What's the ruckus?" a voice growled—Pace's voice.

Shamrock waited for an answer, feeling his palms sweat. If the kid gave it away, then Lobell would toss caution to the winds and move the kid in the night—or shoot him.

Shamrock heard footsteps coming toward him.

"You, kid," Pace said. "That was you yellin'. What do you want?"

"Aw, lemme alone," Maginnis growled sleepily.

"You—say, where'd the matches—" A boot scraped. "Freed! Get . . ."

Shamrock waited for no more. He slipped off the barrel and drifted back into the darkness of the alley. It looked as if Maginnis would keep his mouth shut, but he was only a kid. If Pace and Freed worked him over, he might be beaten into revealing the name of the man at the back window. Shamrock cursed softly.

No. Lobell wouldn't dare touch the kid with Shamrock already suspicious. But it was certain Pace would camp in the cell corridor the rest of the night.

He leaned against an outbuilding, watching the head of the alley. Presently Freed appeared, gun in hand, and lighted a match. He saw the barrel, stared at it for several moments, then at the window. The match died, and Freed lighted another. Then he threw it away and disappeared toward the office.

That cinches it, Shamrock thought disgustedly. Even if Maginnis would open up, Shamrock couldn't get to him now. He cursed the kid's stubbornness. What *was* it he had almost said when Freed buffaloed him? *That's the way he got my—* My what?

Shamrock squatted on his heels in the dark. A fifteen-year-old kid. Why did Lobell want him? To keep something quiet, Shamrock guessed, but what? And there was only one way to keep the kid from talking to anyone—and that was to kill him. Suddenly, Shamrock saw it.

"So that's it," he said softly. Lobell had said Maginnis

was wanted in the next county. Obviously, he wasn't, but Lobell, sticking to his story, would send Maginnis over in care of two gunmen from the sheriff's office. The kid wouldn't be expected in Sahuaro County, so if he didn't show up, no questions would be asked. Even if there were, Lobell would always have the excuse that Maginnis was shot while trying to escape. The *leya del Fuega*—the law of flight—the refuge of every crooked sheriff between the Rio Grande and the Milk River ridge.

It would be easy. Shamrock would be the only outsider who knew Maginnis had been arrested. And tomorrow morning Shamrock would be riding with Lobell out to the Double Diamond. While they were gone, Maginnis would be taken by a couple of sheriff's men. And when Shamrock got back, it would be too late, for Maginnis would be lying in a dry gulch—coyote bait.

Shamrock felt his face go hot at the thought. The kid's only crime had been to find work in the town under a different name, because the name Maginnis was dangerous. In an unguarded moment, he had let slip to Shamrock his real name, and Shamrock had innocently used it to Lobell. And now the kid was slated for a gulching.

He rolled a cigarette and, eyes on the alley mouth, lighted it. He thought of tomorrow. If he stayed in town to keep an eye on Maginnis, Lobell would ride out to the Double Diamond without him. Even if the sheriff didn't down Hyatt, there would be a fight, and the fight would give Lobell the excuse for raising a posse. If Shamrock went out with Lobell, then Maginnis, friendless and unknown, would be taken out and killed.

"Like hell he will," Shamrock said softly.

If he could only make certain that Maginnis would remain in jail until he got back and could watch things, then it would work out. But how to do it and still leave Lobell thinking he suspected nothing?

If he could get the cell key, then Maginnis would have to stay in jail until he could be sawed out. And that would take a half day anyway, working with the tool steel in the bars. By that time Shamrock could be back in town. He'd have to take a chance on Lobell having only one set of keys.

But the keys were in the jail, guarded by Pace and Freed, a couple of capable if uninspired hardcases. And these same keys would have to be got without either Pace or Freed knowing who took them. Impossible.

But was it? Shamrock threw away his cigarette and walked back to the jail. As he approached the barrel, he stopped and took off his boots, so as to diminish the crunch of the cinders. He listened beside the barrel a moment, then crawled up on it. Taking his Stetson off, he edged his head over the sill. Inside, he could see Pace sitting on a back-tilted chair placed just to one side of the corridor door. Freed lounged in the corridor doorway, talking to him.

The lantern was on the floor, and a shotgun lay across Pace's lap. The big wire key ring containing the cell keys was looped over the back of his straight-backed chair. A saddle catalogue lay on the floor beside Pace. Evidently, he was settled for the night.

Shamrock stayed just long enough to stamp the arrangement in his mind, then he climbed down, put his boots on, and crossed the street to the alley.

He seated himself against one of the outbuildings where he could watch the sheriff's office. It was still lighted, and he waited twenty minutes until the light was extinguished. That would be Freed going to bed on the cot.

Shamrock waited a good half hour before he moved again. Then he walked down to the main street, crossed to the sheriff's office, and paused on the corner. The Legal Tender was still lighted, but it was not noisy. The rest of the town was dark.

He turned down the side street again, this time walking softly. At the street door to the office, he paused, and cautiously palmed the knob. The door was unlocked. Slowly he inched it open until there was a foot-wide gap. Then he listened and there came to him the rhythmic breathing of Freed on the cot.

He paused a moment longer, recalling the arrangement of the sparse furniture in the office.

Then he stepped inside and closed the door after him, holding his breath. Freed's breathing was uninterrupted. As his eyes became accustomed to the black of the room, Shamrock saw that the steel corridor door was open a few inches, letting the faint glow of the lantern throw a dim shaft of light on the far wall. His impulse was to take his boots off, but he decided against it, since in case of a hurried retreat stocking feet would be a handicap.

Stealthily he made his way across the room, pausing every few feet to listen. When he reached the corridor door, he was less than three feet from the cot, and he could make out Freed's head. Freed was facing the wall, his back to Shamrock, but Shamrock knew when he opened the corridor door more light would be thrown on Freed. It was a small thing but it might wake him.

Shamrock was casting around for Freed's clothes when his gaze happened to fall to the floor. There, in the crack of the corridor door, lay Freed's Levi's.

Shamrock picked them up and, holding the corridor door with one hand, he placed the Levi's almost against Freed's head, arranging them gently so they would block out all light in case Freed turned over.

When it was done, he paused again. Freed's breathing had turned into a soft snore, and Shamrock cursed. If Freed was snoring and the door was opened, the increase in the volume of noise might warn Pace. So Shamrock waited.

He waited ten minutes until Freed stirred a little and

ceased his snoring.

Then with infinite slowness, Shamrock pulled the steel door back. One squeak of metal on metal in this profound silence would be as loud as the crack of doom, and Pace was just inside the door. It took him ten minutes to get the door open enough to give him body room. Cautiously he edged his head through the crack and looked.

The lantern was on the floor, maybe five feet from him. The jail, added on to the sheriff's office, was of triple-thick adobe brick, so that the walls were perhaps three feet through.

Pace was immediately to the left of the entrance, and Shamrock saw with quiet exultation that he had not moved. He had counted on that. There had not been enough room for Pace's chair in the setback between the doorway and the cells, so that it projected out a little. The back frame that held the keys was free of the wall, in plain sight, as were the keys. They could be lifted easily as long as Pace was occupied.

Shamrock looked at the floor for any sand or gravel. He saw none, and he put his foot out, letting his weight settle cautiously on the boards. They did not creak.

Then he stepped through the door and flattened himself against the wall. He was holding his breath, every muscle straining for quiet.

Not a sound so far. Cautiously he reached out for the ring. If he could keep the keys from jangling, then he would be safe.

Crash!

Even in that instant of sound, Shamrock knew what had happened. The door behind him had slammed.

He kicked out at the light, at the same time whipping up his gun in a high arc and lunging for Pace's back.

Pace, in the act of swiveling his head, took the down-sweeping barrel square on top of his Stetson as the light went out and the lantern clattered across the floor.

Shamrock grabbed the keys as he heard Pace slide out of his chair and slump on the floor.

Keys in hand, he whirled. If he was quick, he could get out before Freed was fully awake.

He felt frantically for the doorknob. Where it should have been was smooth sheet steel.

Then he understood. The inside, of course, had no knob or latch. A safety device to make a jail break harder. That's why the door had been wedged open with the Levi's.

He was trapped.

Grimly he fought down his panic and listened. Freed would be wakened. Would he understand the truth, or would he, fogged by sleep, think a draft had slammed it?

He listened.

"Pace," a thick voice called from outside. It was Freed. How did Pace talk? "Yeah. Open up," Shamrock mouthed gruffly.

Then he listened. If Freed had a light, he was lost.

He heard a fumbling with the lock. He holstered his gun, put a hand on each doorway wall to brace him, and raised a foot.

The door swung open—on a dark room. Freed's body bulked large in the gloom.

"Whatsa'—"

Shamrock put all his weight behind his shoving foot that settled in Freed's belly and kited him off across the room.

Without waiting for more, Shamrock streaked through the door, across the office, and out the street door, just as he heard Freed crash into some furniture. He ran straight across the street for the alley, and in its welcome darkness stopped.

He saw a match flare in the office. That would be Freed.

Shamrock about-faced and raced down the alley, turning

in at the hotel. The rope was still hanging from the window and he pulled himself up hand over hand. In another minute, he was in his own room undressing in the dark.

In yet another minute, he was in bed, the key ring under his pillow, his Colt on the covers.

He waited a long five minutes, then he heard footsteps on the stairs.

When the knock came on his door, he called sleepily, "Yeah?"

"Open up!"

"Come in careful," Shamrock said warningly, getting out of bed and backing against the wall. The bed was mussed, his hair was tousled, and his gun was trained on the door when it swung open.

It was Freed, Pace, and the clerk.

"See?" the clerk said righteously to Pace. "He's been here nigh on to two hours."

"What is this?" Shamrock growled.

Pace's pale, shallow eyes glared at him suspiciously, then looked at the bed.

"Nothin'," he said.

Shamrock glared back. "I'll give you five seconds to clear the hell outa here."

Hurriedly, Freed backed out the door, the clerk crowding him. Pace, more sullen, took his time.

The door slammed on Shamrock's mental count of five. He shot once into the door.

As the echo died, he heard the receding clamor of footsteps racing down the hall.

He climbed back in bed and immediately went to sleep.

CHAPTER EIGHT

It was the beginning of a perfect spring day when Shamrock stepped out onto the street next morning. It was early, so he was in no particular hurry as he went into Sanford's General Store and bought a couple of boxes of forty-five shells with which he filled the gaps in his shell belt—six of them. The rest he emptied into his handkerchief and rammed into his hip pocket.

His breakfast at the café was leisurely. Halfway through it, he looked up to see Freed enter. They glared at each other, then Shamrock went on unhurriedly with his meal. Finished, he rolled a cigarette, stepped out into the street, and turned down to the sheriff's office. Before he reached the corner, all the expression had gone from his face, leaving it dead, yet curiously alert. If Lobell suspected him of the jail assault, the showdown would be fast and deadly.

Six horses were at the hitchrack, Blue among them. That meant the sheriff's picked gunmen were all in the office. Shamrock walked up to Blue, slapped his shoulder affectionately, and noted with misgiving that the reins were tied in a secure, elaborate knot to the hitchrail. Was it an omen?

He swung under the hitchrack onto the walk and stepped into the office. Lobell was seated at the desk, the other three men in chairs around the room.

His entry was greeted with silence. He looked insolently at Lobell, then his stare traveled the room.

"Howdy," Lobell said tonelessly.

Shamrock dragged his gaze from the sullen face of Pace, who was looking a bit pale.

"What are we waitin' for?" Shamrock asked.

"Freed. He's eatin'."

Shamrock shoved some papers aside and sat down on the edge of the desk. He carefully refrained from looking at the closed corridor door while he built a smoke with deliberate and steady fingers. He guessed that Freed by this time was making a thorough search of his room for the missing key ring, and he smiled inwardly as he felt the keys press against him where they were rolled tightly in two bandannas and tied about his waist. The ring was under the door of a vacant room.

Finished with his cigarette, he calmly observed Lobell's recruits. He wondered if the ranchers of Santa Rita slope were so green they didn't know Lobell was hiring gunmen for deputies, or if they didn't care. The small man of the affair in the stables last night was here. He was Harmer, Shamrock remembered. He was dressed in blue Levi's and shirt a little more soiled than ordinary, and wore a flat-crowned Stetson pulled low over his lack of forehead. He was frail-looking, but Shamrock knew that was deceptive, knew that his kind lived on whisky and danger until one or both downed him.

The other man was a stranger, well-fed, almost fat, with an amiable blankness of face that was close to idiocy. Both wore guns within easy reach, even when seated.

Shamrock, finished with his examination, laughed quietly. "Are these the—good men?" he asked Lobell. The sheriff nodded.

"Talk to 'em. They ain't happy."

Harmer stirred uneasily and cleared his throat, but did not take his eyes from Shamrock.

"Somethin' happened last night," Lobell said.

"It must have," Shamrock replied.

The sheriff studied him closely, a suggestion of a smile playing on his dignified features.

"Someone busted in here last night and got the cell keys."

Shamrock received the news with a slight frown. "In here? How?" he asked, his tone one of disbelief, of mild though distant surprise.

"I dunno. I wasn't here."

"Who was it?"

"That's what we'd like to know."

Shamrock looked at him a moment, puzzled. Then slowly his gaze shuttled over to Pace.

"I see," he said softly.

Pace's stare faded away and he evaded Shamrock's glare.

"See what?" the sheriff asked.

Shamrock ignored him, and spoke to Pace. "If I'd known that, you stuffed Stetson, I'd of got you out quicker."

"Known what?" the sheriff said.

Shamrock stared at him insolently. "Cut it, Lobell. Two of them trained hooligans of yours swarmed in my room in the middle of the night like a call for free drinks." He looked over at Pace. "You wise slob," he said quietly.

"Now wait," Lobell put in patiently. "Pace ain't said a thing."

Shamrock made an unprintable sound, and leaned back against the wall.

"Whoever it was," the sheriff continued evenly, "slugged Pace, grabbed the keys, give Freed a kick in the guts, and run."

"Good."

"It was just too bad," the sheriff continued, observing Shamrock closely. "Just too damn bad. We got another set, but I'd sure like to know who it was."

Not a muscle in Shamrock's face moved. "Why don't you give up and start searchin' each other?" and he laughed quietly at the flush crawling up the sheriff's neck.

Lobell sat back in his chair. "That face," he said softly.

"Some day it's goin' to get you in trouble—bad trouble."

A step sounded in the doorway and a man strode in. He was an old man, with a grimed face and dirty overalls. In his hand was a hacksaw and a dozen blades. Two men were behind him.

"Let's have a look at it," he said bluntly. "This tool steel is hell to cut, though."

The sheriff, caught in his own lie, looked up at Shamrock uncomfortably. "The end cell on the left, John. Start on it."

The old man—the blacksmith, Shamrock guessed—stomped over to the corridor door and went inside. The other men lounged into the room, looked quickly at Shamrock and then at the sheriff. Two more of the sheriff's hardcases.

"Help him," Lobell ordered them curtly.

These were the two Lobell had counted on to take Maginnis out, Shamrock thought as they filed into the jail.

A moment later Freed entered, and the sheriff rose.

"You all got carbines?" he asked them.

They nodded, all except Shamrock.

"Have you?" Lobell asked him.

"I never use one," Shamrock replied, and lounged off the desk.

Two minutes later, they had crossed the bridge and were walking their horses up the hill opposite town. When they reached the top, the sheriff in front set a stiff, workmanlike pace toward the north and the Double Diamond.

He wisely cut across country, choosing the screening mesquite and sage rather than the traveled trails. His riders conversed little among themselves and then only to borrow matches or give directions. It was a grim and businesslike cavalcade, and Shamrock knew their instructions had been given them already. Each man carried a gun and double belts, one of them for carbine shells.

The sheriff's air was one of eager though doubtful antici-
pation, and he did not talk much. Occasionally he would
covertly observe Shamrock, but Shamrock was his usual
self—taciturn, arrogant, almost indifferent.

Lobell did not stop until they swung onto the Double
Diamond road just before it topped the ridge and dropped
into the steep-sided basin where the ranch lay. Then he
reined up and his men drew up around him.

"This is your idea," he said to Shamrock. "What do you
aim to do?"

Shamrock crooked a leg over the horn and replied lazily,
"He'll be expecting us and he'll likely be forted up in the
house or the bunkhouse. Call him out and give him
warnin' that you've come to take possession. Ain't that it?"

The sheriff nodded agreement.

"If he won't go, then we'll ride in. If he shoots, that's
all you want, isn't it, Lobell?"

The sheriff was a little long in answering. "Is it?"

Shamrock shrugged. "It'll give you a chance to smoke
him out."

"All right," the sheriff said pleasantly. "Let's go."

Lobell and Shamrock rode in the vanguard. As their
horses took the downgrade, Lobell looked up over the
valley to the ranch on the other side. They saw someone
leave the house and walk swiftly toward the bunkhouse.

"They've seen us," he said.

Shamrock paid no attention to him. He was wondering
if Hyatt would have the sense to see the difference between
six men and a posse. He had told Shamrock he intended
to first warn the sheriff off the place, then, when the posse
arrived, fight it out. Shamrock counted on his keeping his
word, but above all he hoped Hyatt would have the sense
to detect an ambush and keep under cover.

He was wondering, too, just how much longer he could
run with both the hare and the hounds.

CHAPTER NINE

THE DOUBLE DIAMOND lay deserted in the warm morning sunshine. Not a horse was in the corral, and the far barns looked like squat and sleepy beetles in the sun. The bunkhouse, then, directly in front of the gate across sixty yards of corral lot, was to be the fort. Its broad side faced them, and the door was shut, the windows out.

Even the gate was open. Shamrock reined Blue over to go through when a shot whanged out from the bunkhouse and kicked up dirt at Blue's feet.

"That's far enough!" a voice called.

The sheriff looked briefly at Shamrock.

"Call him out," Shamrock said.

Lobell called to the bunkhouse. "Hyatt!"

"Yeah?" Matt answered.

"Come out here."

"You come in here," Matt's voice replied. "You, Lobell —alone."

Again the sheriff looked at Shamrock.

"Go on in," Shamrock gibed.

Lobell laughed harshly. "I'd get a slug in my belly before I was halfway there. Get him out here."

As Shamrock had foreseen, the brunt of the business was to fall on his shoulders. Lobell expected him to get Hyatt out, so they could talk, finally quarrel, and kill Hyatt in the gunplay.

"Send your men off, then," Shamrock suggested. "He might come out."

The sheriff considered a moment, then shook his head. He wanted Hyatt badly, but he had no stomach for facing

81

him alone. "I won't let him near me when I'm alone. He'd cut me to doll rags. I got him on the run. Why should I give him a chance to take me with him? Huh-uh."

"You got to warn him," Shamrock insisted. "Go ahead and shout, then."

Lobell was about to open his mouth when he caught the mocking, jeering expression on Shamrock's face. He paused, surveying Shamrock speculatively. "Maybe you'd like to go. Maybe you can get him to come out and make medicine."

Without a word, Shamrock slid out of the saddle and started through the gate. He was ten feet into the corral lot when a shot from the bunkhouse kicked dirt at his feet.

"Tell Lobell to come along!" a voice called.

Shamrock did not even pause in his lazy, casual, self-assured stride. The second shot was closer still, but he went on. He was looking at the bunkhouse. In the four windows of its long side, eight rifles stuck through.

"Go back and send Lobell!" a voice called. This time it was Hyatt's.

Still Shamrock came on. He was sweating a little. The end rifle cracked, and Shamrock felt something tug at his shirt. He looked down casually and saw a hole in his shirt low at his side near his waistline. Still he walked on, his stride deliberate but sweat beading his forehead. He was close now, maybe fifty feet from the bunkhouse.

"Stop right there!" Matt's voice ordered him sharply.

Shamrock pulled up.

"Say it from there."

Shamrock looked at the windows. All the rifles had been withdrawn and the square window holes yawned blackly at him. How many men had a bead on the Durham tag on his shirt?

He put his hands on his hips. "Unless you're damn

fools," he said so softly that Lobell could not possibly over-hear him, "you'll let me in. Don't speak loud."

There was a murmur of voices from inside the building, then Hyatt said quietly, "Come in."

Shamrock walked straight for the door. He heard it being unbarred and he walked in and closed it behind him.

There, rifles in hand, facing him were four people; Nancy, Matt, Hyatt, and a lone puncher. That was why they hadn't wanted him to come in, because they were so few. Shamrock leaned against the door, feeling the hostility in their stares—and the look of stubbornness and determination, which he hated more.

"The sheriff's pet gunman," Matt said quietly.

"Hyatt, I'm talkin' to you," Shamrock said. "If you got a head on you, you'll listen."

Hyatt's gun was slacked on his forearm. He leaned on the long table under which Shamrock could see cases of rifle shells and more guns. Even the fatigue in Hyatt's eyes couldn't hide their smoldering anger, and the muscles were corded along his jaw line. In the half gloom of the bunkhouse, he looked just what he was—a man calm but desperate in the knowledge that he was fighting for something already lost.

"Get it over with."

"Give up. You haven't got a chance."

"What did I say, Mayo?" Nancy asked coldly. "Didn't I tell you?"

"You better go, Ireland," Hyatt said shortly.

"Think a minute. Your ranch is going whether you live or die. Can't you savvy that?"

"Too dang well," Matt murmured.

"If you're dead, you'll never win it back."

"And I won't worry about who took it," Hyatt said.

"Lobell's comin' back," Shamrock continued doggedly. "If it hadn't been for me, he'd be out there with a posse now. I got him out here by tellin' him he'd likely have the chance of killing you in the argument. But if you run him off, he'll be back with the posse tomorrow." He looked around him. "Three men and a woman. You can't even put up a sizable scrap."

"What's your cut out of all this?" Nancy asked scornfully.

Shamrock ignored her. "Will you give up and high-tail it to the mountains?" he asked Hyatt.

"No."

"All right," Shamrock said, and he walked over to the table, picked up a carbine, and moved over so he could see through a window. They watched him curiously as he stacked shell cases on the table. Then he walked around to the other side of it, laid the gun across the top case for a steady aim, and bent forward to sight it. Hyatt, first to act, jumped in front of the gun.

"What're you doin', Ireland?"

"I'm goin' to kill Lobell."

"Kill him?" Matt asked incredulously.

"I'm throwin' in with you folks," Shamrock said indifferently. "If we got to die, there's no sense in lettin' that polecat take the pot."

The girl walked slowly over to her brother and looked quickly at him, then her puzzled gaze settled on Shamrock.

"You mean it?" she asked slowly.

"If you'll get out of the way, I aim to show you."

Hyatt bent his head and rubbed his forehead and face with his hand. "God!" he said hoarsely. "We can't do it. We can't do it."

"Is—is it that hopeless?" Nancy asked. The fear in her voice balled something up in Shamrock.

"You know the country. I've got your word for what the cattlemen will do," Shamrock said. "But I know Lobell—better than any of you do, I reckon. He's out to wolf you, and he'll do it. Nothin' can stop him. If you're goin' to fight, you might as well start now by knockin' him over. It's not pretty, but neither's his game."

"Why are you doing this—siding with us?" Nancy asked.

Shamrock's eyes were opaque as he looked at her. "I'm just a killer," he said dryly. "I like the smell of blood. I like to kill people. I'd like to kill Lobell." Then his voice dropped its jeering and he added, "I'd like to kill some of these stuffed galluses that won't give a man a chance to live his own life."

"There you've hit it," Matt said.

Shamrock observed Hyatt quietly. "There's no law says I can't buy into this fight, is there?"

Hyatt said nothing, did not move.

"Then get out of the way," Shamrock said, leaning over his gun. "This is my first ante."

Hyatt looked briefly, eloquently, at Nancy.

"I reckon you're right, Ireland," Hyatt said dully. "I was so damn sure I was, but I wasn't. We've been loco. The thing to do if we're going to fight him in the end is to kill him now—use his own trick—but I can't do it. I won't."

"Let him do it," Nancy said passionately. "We're going to kill Lobell anyway."

"No," Hyatt said grimly. "I won't."

"I hate it, too," Nancy said in a low voice, "but it's Lobell or us. It may be the only chance we'll get, Mayo."

"I'll give up first. I'm going to. I'll ride out."

"You won't give up," Shamrock said softly. "You've been an outlaw, Hyatt, but never the outlaw you will be from now on. Take to the dodge. Play a slow, waitin' game, watchin' him until you can step in and catch him and hang him so high the buzzards can't reach him."

Nancy turned on him, eyes blazing. "You fool! Can't you see that's what they want him to do! Can't you see they want him to turn outlaw so they can hunt him down!"

"If he won't, he can die here like a hero," Shamrock said coldly. "What will it get you?"

"But it won't work! It can't work!" She turned pleading eyes on Mayo. "Are you going back to that hunted life, an outcast to me—to all of us? Isn't it better to stay here and fight until some of them see reason? You were lucky once, Mayo, but it won't hold twice! Listen to him and we're lost!"

"It may be a hunted life," Shamrock said dryly, "but at least he'll be alive. Keep him here and they'll kill him."

"But it won't happen! It can't! We'll send for the governor's help! Aren't there men somewhere that won't stand by and see it happen?" Nancy cried passionately.

"You're fightin' the law," Shamrock jeered, "and the law says you're wrong. So it'll swear in forty nice peaceable family men to shoot and burn! And when they're done, the Hyatts and the Hyatts' spread will be just a bloody memory."

"And Mayo submits to that or turns outlaw?" Nancy asked quietly.

"Unless he wants to take up a homestead and brood. Do you think he will?"

"Stop it!" Hyatt commanded. He turned to Nancy. "Sis, I've tried to stick by our agreement—to stay put here on the ranch and not fight. But they won't mix. Either we let Lobell call out a mob and kill us off, or we run. Peace won't do it. To hell with my parole! Out there I'll still have a chance to save the spread. Here I'll die like a rat—and leave you alone. I won't do it."

He turned to Shamrock. "Go out and tell Lobell the place is his—every log, nail, pole, and board in it—even the food. By noon, we'll be headed for the mountains."

Shamrock's face settled into its sleepy alertness as he laid down the carbine. "That's sense. Where do you aim to go?"

"Don't tell him, Mayo," Nancy put in quickly. She had been watching Shamrock with that cold distaste with which a woman watches a man who has been fighting her emotion with logic, and winning. And now she said slowly to him, "It was all a bluff, wasn't it? It was all planned out to get us to leave, to give Lobell a free hand. I wouldn't trust that sneering face of yours if I saw it in heaven!"

"Nancy!" Hyatt said.

But Nancy was staring at Shamrock. "Can you look me in the eye and say you didn't lie, that you didn't bluff, that you aren't doing this for money?"

"Yes," Shamrock answered promptly and he looked at her evenly, his gray eyes unblinking.

It was Nancy's gaze that dropped first, and she turned away with a choking sob. Matt folded her into his arms.

"Why are men so hard, so damned, *damned* unreasonable?" she said into Matt's shoulder. Matt smiled at Shamrock over her head.

Shamrock said to Hyatt, "Where will you be?"

"Then you're still throwing in with us?"

Shamrock nodded.

"The Notch is the best place, Mayo," Matt said. "He can't miss it."

Hyatt nodded. "We'll be up there, Ireland. Straight west and a little south, clear up in the peaks. You can see it from town. It's a deep cut in the Ritas. You'll be able to pick up our sign there."

Shamrock loosened his gun and looked at the door. He was still a moment, then he said, "Don't any of you come out of here until long after we've rode off, will you? And you, Hyatt, if anybody calls to you, don't answer."

He opened the door and stood on the steps. His sinister bluff about shooting Lobell had worked, had made them see the insanity of their stubbornness in staying. Hyatt had done the only thing he knew, torn between forfeiting his parole and his passion to keep the spread. And Nancy, blind to everything, had held him to it to the last. And she thought Shamrock was a hireling of Lobell's. Would she if she could understand how he was beating his brains to find a way now to face Lobell? For Shamrock knew that it would take magnificent bluffing, an iron nerve to face the sheriff now.

With a still, cold face, he started across the corral lot.

All five of them were facing him, mounted, watchful, as he approached.

"Where is he?" Lobell asked.

Shamrock swung onto Blue before he answered. Then he looked deliberately at Lobell, the mockery in his eyes little dancing lights.

"He give up," Shamrock said. "If you come back in an hour, the place is yours."

Lobell didn't say anything for a full ten seconds, then he said, "Well, isn't that fine? How many men are in there?"

"Ten," Shamrock said, looking the sheriff in the eye.

The sheriff thought a moment. "Countin' Hyatt?"

"Did I say Hyatt?" Shamrock asked softly. "I didn't mean to. He's not there." He spoke the lie deliberately, with obvious enjoyment.

The sheriff came erect in his saddle, then he leaned forward, all the false good humor gone from his face. "Not there, did you say?"

For answer, Shamrock turned in the saddle so he could survey the men behind him. "Hyatt was tipped off that we were comin' out here this mornin'. And if I don't miss my guess plenty, he knew *why* we were comin'. He's gone, high-tailed it. His foreman's in there ready to pay off the hands. Give him time to leave, he says, and the place is ours." He paused, his gaze still on the other men. "Somebody has been talkin'," he said meaningfully.

Each of the four looked at the others, then at the sheriff, then at Shamrock.

"I thought I heard Hyatt's voice," Pace said bluntly.

"I thought I did, too," Shamrock answered, and let it go at that.

The sheriff was looking over his men, and Shamrock tried to keep from holding his breath until Lobell spoke. Shamrock was sure Pace and Freed had been told last night of the plans to down Hyatt, and maybe the other two had. He was staking everything on that chance.

Then Lobell said, "So that's it? Somebody has been gettin' ideas." His voice was smooth and deadly.

"I'd of swore that was Hyatt walkin' to the bunkhouse when we was comin' down that far hill," Pace persisted.

"Go in and see," Shamrock invited. "There's that foreman in there just honin' to see you—any of you, but Lobell especially. They want to thank you for bein' out of a job."

"Nothin' happened to you," Pace blustered.

Shamrock said nothing. He knew Pace was calculating his chances of getting through the same welcome Shamrock did, and he knew, too, that Pace's kind found courage only in numbers. And now Pace fell silent in the face of Lobell's cool stare. Of all of them, Harmer was the calmest. He was almost indifferent, yet he met Lobell's look in kind, and did not shift his gaze.

"Let's go," Lobell said briefly.

Shamrock immediately turned Blue in to side the sheriff. The others, in the order of their coming, turned and started down the road, Pace and Harmer in the lead.

"It's funny, ain't it," the sheriff said suddenly, "that you can save some men's necks a dozen times, but if you call on 'em for a little gratitude, they sell out for a drink."

None of them spoke, and the sheriff mused on, but this time in silence. They had gone a mile before Lobell asked, "Where'd Hyatt get all the men? Five in their crew."

"I saw one of them in the Legal Tender last night," Shamrock lied.

"Gunman?"

"Looked it."

The sheriff was quiet awhile. "When did Hyatt leave?"

"Last night," Shamrock said carelessly.

They were slogging down the trail, each of them tense and wary when Lobell turned suddenly to Shamrock. "Last night, you say. Are you sure of that?"

"The foreman said so."

Lobell lapsed into silence again, yet Shamrock wondered. He was about to risk a question, then decided against it.

"Did you ever mention this Maginnis to Hyatt?" the sheriff asked presently.

Shamrock looked blankly at him. "No. Why should I?"

"So *that's* it," the sheriff said softly.

The sheriff's face was strangely composed. Shamrock cast about for a clue to Lobell's reasoning, but he could not find it.

It was scarcely a minute until the sheriff's horse shied a little, skitting out to the side of the road. He cursed him gently, and the men, who had looked back, turned around again to their business.

Shamrock saw it. With a deadly swift, near-invisible flick of his hand the sheriff whipped his gun up and shot. The slug hit Pace in the back and he was driven over the horn of his saddle; then he slipped off into the road.

Before the rest could quiet their horses, the sheriff had them covered. They all stopped, Shamrock included, looking stupidly at the sheriff, then at Pace.

He was lying face down in the dust, a hole in his back.

"The next time one of you thinks you can sell me out, remember that," the sheriff said pleasantly. He looked over at Freed. "I don't think you were in it, Freed. I don't know, but I don't think so."

Freed licked his lips nervously. "I—I don't savvy it, Andy."

"After we took that Maginnis kid in, George and Harmer took Coyne's body over to the hardware store. Freed, you took them horses back to the stable. Ireland and me was in the Legal Tender. Comin' out here for Hyatt was his idea. After I left him, I went back and told Pace about it. Then I went down to see Coyne. Everybody was busy—except Pace." He laughed softly. "He was the only man free.

"He skipped out and told one of Hyatt's men that we'd caught Maginnis. Hyatt was in town somewhere and Pace told him. Hyatt staged that key grab. And Pace helped him. Hyatt didn't carry a gun because he knew if another murder was hung on him, the county would string him up. It would have gone off good, except that door slammed and he didn't have time to talk to Maginnis." He spoke to Freed now. "They knew it would wake you, Freed, so Pace give his head a hell of a bump to make it look like he was slugged, and Hyatt high-tailed it past you." He paused a moment, regarding Freed coldly. "Of course, Pace could have bought you in on it when you got back. It's damn funny a man could sneak into that jail with you in it."

"I—I done a lot of things, but I ain't crossed you yet, Andy," Freed said surlily.

Lobell holstered his gun. "I don't suppose a one of you knows what this means?"

No one spoke.

"It means Hyatt is likely in town now with a gang of men and that he's yanked Maginnis clean out of jail." His voice was harsh with anger. "Ride, dammit! Ride. Don't stare at me! Ride!"

Lobell roweled his horse into the lead, leaving the road and taking off across country at a gallop. The rest followed, reining around Pace's still body, face down in the dust. Shamrock was content to remain in the rear, only a dogged determination to see this through preventing him from riding up and blasting Lobell out of his saddle. Shamrock's blind, artless lying had caused Pace's death, but then Pace was slated to die by violence anyway. Only the manner of it angered Shamrock.

And as he rode, Shamrock pigeonholed a few more facts. Maginnis, alive, was of the greatest importance to Hyatt, although Hyatt didn't know it. And Maginnis, dead, was what the sheriff wanted—and seemed likely to get. Shamrock didn't doubt now that his theft of the keys had saved the youngster's life.

And one other fact had been revealed, a fact that Shamrock had guessed at his first meeting with Lobell. The sheriff was a gunman. He had the genius for handling a gun and the will to kill when he was crossed. And that, Shamrock knew, made him as deadly as a rattlesnake with wings.

All Shamrock's cunning and deception could go on only so long, then he would face that gun, and try to match it. His ruse had worked this time, and he had pulled Lobell away from the spread, but a showdown was coming. And that was all right, too.

CHAPTER TEN

LOBELL, IN SPITE OF HIS BULK, was first off his horse at the rack in front of the sheriff's office. Shamrock was a close second.

Lobell strode into the office, yanked open the corridor door—on the blacksmith patiently working over his saw.

One bar was out. The second was sawed through at the top and almost through at the bottom. Maginnis sat inside, watching the work with a white, tensed face, sliding occasional glances at the two gunmen who were helping the blacksmith. He was fighting to keep the fear out of his face, but it was evident to Shamrock that he was afraid.

Lobell said casually, "Nobody been here, eh?"

The two helpers shook their heads. Maginnis was looking at Shamrock over the sheriff's shoulder, and Shamrock let the trace of a smile play on his face and shook his head.

"That's fine," Lobell said genially. "How long will it be?"

One of the helpers looked at Shamrock, then at Lobell. "About an hour, I reckon."

"Like hell," the blacksmith said, not even stopping the saw.

Lobell plucked his lip judiciously, as if debating with himself. "Well, take your time, John. It ain't sense startin' out on a long trip in the middle of the afternoon. I don't aim to have you boys travel at night with a prisoner, and you could hardly make it to any ranch by dark. Better wait till tomorrow."

Shamrock followed Lobell back into the office. The others were waiting for the sheriff, and he slacked into a chair with obvious relief.

His first act was to slip a peppermint into his mouth and suck on it a moment, rolling it around in his mouth with simple relish. "That's a heap of worry off my mind." He sighed. Sitting there, he looked like some benevolent grandfather fretting over a summer hay crop. Shamrock found it hard to believe that only an hour or so since, Lobell had shot a man in the back—shot him because he had been panicked into it.

Lobell rolled a smoke deliberately, then reached in a drawer for papers and addressed Harmer. "Harmer, you take them horses down to the stable. If Huston ain't found out yet what become of his help, you tell him. Tell him to put Ireland's blue on the county bill, too. George, you go over to Skelly and find out when Coyne will be ready for buryin'." Here he looked at Shamrock, and Shamrock thought he saw faintly veiled amusement in those agate-blue eyes. "Freed, you got Pace's job." He paused significantly. "I hope you got better sense than he had."

Then he looked at Shamrock almost fondly. "You, son, high-tail it down to the courthouse and git me the assessed valuation on Morgan's Fryin' Pan outfit. It's up for sale and I got to git the notices off to the printer on tonight's stage. You see Pinckney; he's the assessor. If he ain't got it, prod him into it. Wait for it if you have to."

He stood up. "Me, I'm goin' over to the bank and tell 'em they got the Double Diamond."

Shamrock, as the sheriff talked, had been listening to the rapid grating of the saw. He could tell by the dogged insistence of its tone that Maginnis's span in jail would be short. Lobell was sending him off on some petty job to get him out of the way, and it was on his lips to refuse with his customary insolence. Caution checked him, however, and he rose with a nod and left the building.

He started for Blue when the sheriff spoke from the door. "It ain't a far piece, son—just up the street."

"Oh," Shamrock said noncommittally, and turned in the direction the sheriff was pointing. Silently, he cursed himself. That was a blundering that might rouse the sheriff's suspicion, but it was done.

The single cross street of Malpais Springs crossed the bridge to the north, stopped at the bottom of a hill slope to the south. To the south of the main street behind the business buildings, the frame houses of the townsmen roosted, most of them on the cross street. Midway between the main street and the hill stood the courthouse.

It was a square adobe affair and lay off the street, surrounded by a bare, hardpacked dirt yard, a long hitchrack and watering trough and a single cottonwood on one side, a horse shed, a large corral, and other outbuildings on the other.

Rains of a decade had cut and gnawed into its walls, so that great sheets of the mud coating had fallen away, exposing the sun-dried bricks. Cardboard stopped the weather in most of the four front windows, and four or five flimsy bars proclaimed that it had once served as the jail, too.

From its steps, Shamrock could still see the jail. On the other side of the street far down, skulking idly in the shade trees, Shamrock could see Harmer, sent by Lobell to keep an eye on him until Maginnis was removed from jail. The four corners were quiet. Shamrock stepped into the corridor and immediately went to a side window where he could see the corral. A bay and a sorrel were standing hipshot, cheek-to-rump, stomping flies.

Then he turned into the first door he came to. It let into a littered office. Tilted back in a chair, his feet on the desk, his hands flat on the chair arms, his head sunk as if in thought, sat a bald, gaunt man in shirt sleeves—asleep.

Shamrock swept the man's feet off the desk, letting them crash to the floor and lurch their owner erect. The man roused like a mule, wide awake.

"Where's Pinckney?"

"I'm Pinckney," the man said dryly.

Shamrock sized him up a brief moment, then looked around the room. There was a huge, steel-backed door that led into a dark room—a record room, Shamrock judged. From a hasp in the wall by it, a huge padlock dangled.

"You got a key for that?" Shamrock asked, indicating the padlock.

"It's in my office," Pinckney said pompously. "Who

would have if I didn't?"

"Who would?" Shamrock echoed, then added, "Wait a minute."

He left the room and walked to a side window where he could look down at the four corners. There were men and horses in front of the sheriff's office now. They had Maginnis free and were getting ready to ride.

Shamrock looked across the street. There was Harmer, leaning against a tree trunk, watching the courthouse door.

Shamrock walked swiftly out the door, turned to his right, and rounded the corner of the building. He was almost running.

When he was out of Harmer's sight, he dodged in close to the building and flattened out against it, gun in hand.

He had only to wait a few seconds, when Harmer rounded the corner on the run.

He stopped short when he saw Shamrock, saw the gun covering him. They looked at each other a moment, before Shamrock said, "In a hurry?"

"Huh-uh."

"Well, I am." He walked over and took Harmer's gun, then prodded him in the back. "Get in Pinckney's office."

Pinckney was sitting bolt upright as they entered, a look of blank astonishment on his face.

"I'll take that key," Shamrock said coldly.

"But—but what for?"

"I want the padlock key and the key to the office door."

Pinckney stood up, his chest swelling with indignity. Shamrock calmly shoved him back into his chair again, his other hand holding the gun in Harmer's back.

"You want me to take them?" he drawled softly.

"No, but you have no right—I'll report this to the authorities. This is the damnedest insolence I ever witnessed."

Shamrock held out his hand mutely, and Pinckney subsided. He dragged out a key chain and removed two keys from it.

"Now get up!" Shamrock ordered him briefly, and when Pinckney only stared at him, he pointed his gun at him and said, "All right. Maybe I can blow you up."

Immediately Pinckney bounded out of his chair.

"Now get in that room," he ordered, indicating the record room.

"It won't work," Harmer said quietly, sneering. "This'll get it for you—get it plenty."

Shamrock rammed his gun in Pinckney's back and shoved them both toward the door. Harmer went peacefully, Pinckney protesting.

"But, man, we'll smother! There's no air in here! We'll die!"

"I wouldn't be that lucky," Shamrock said.

When they were inside, he swung the heavy door shut, slid the steel bar in place, and padlocked it tightly.

Then he locked the office door, went out to the corral, saddled the bay, and headed west for the hill. At the end of the street there was a trail that climbed the hill, and Shamrock held to it until it lifted a hundred feet or so above the town. He cursed because he didn't have Blue, but it would have been impossible to go back and get him without alarming Lobell.

Halfway up the slope Shamrock reined up and looked back over the town. Although he was not much above it, he could see all the roads leading out. Off to the south, just on the edge of town, beginning to climb out of the pocket of the valley were three horsemen traveling at a smart clip.

He urged the bay on, working doggedly for the top of the rise. There wouldn't be any time to lose, he knew, for as soon as they were far enough from town so the sound of shots wouldn't carry, they would get it over with.

On the ridge, Shamrock looked off south and west. In the middle distance, beyond a dozen low ridges and around the end of a low mesa, he saw the faint pencil line of the wagon road threading west through the rocky foothills.

That would be it. He rammed in the hooks, roweling the surprised bay into a gallop down the slope. It wasn't long before the bay sensed the urgency of his rider, and he stretched out willingly, taking the rough going and climbs with sturdy labor and the open going with a stretching lope. Shamrock didn't spare him, didn't let up on him once until they reached the road.

He dismounted before the bay had skidded to a stop and examined the dust. The most recent tracks were headed toward town. Then he was ahead of them.

He looked at the road curving toward him down the hill. If he waited, he might be too late, and he decided not to chance it. Swinging on the bay again, he headed up the slope.

Approaching them this way, there would be no hope for surprise, but it didn't matter. Surprising them was just another name for ambushing them, and Shamrock didn't care for that. He settled his Colt so it swung free and hung straight.

At the top of the rise, before and below him in the next dip, he saw the three horsemen. It was Maginnis, all right, in the middle. Shamrock jogged his horse down the slope in no particular hurry.

They met at the valley bottom, where the road crossed a dry, sandy arroyo.

The guards were the same two who had been helping the blacksmith, tall, rawboned men both, with the pale hair and eyes, the calm and sturdy insolence of the born Texas gunman.

If they were surprised to see him, they didn't show it. The one on the right, mounted on a roan, looked at his companion.

"Reckon we ought to ride over him, or step around?"

"Let's wrap him up and tote him back to Lobell," the other said. "He 'pears to be in a tol'able hurry."

Shamrock cuffed the Stetson back off his forehead and spat.

"Before you try it," he drawled, "I got somethin' you'd like to see."

"It ain't your face," the first one said.

"What is it?" the second said.

Maginnis said nothing, sitting there white-lipped, hobbled to his stirrups by a rope under the horse's belly. There were handcuffs on his wrists.

"It's around my waist under my shirt," Shamrock said. "I'd get it, but I'm afraid you'd get spooky and I'd have to pull a gun on you."

The taller one smiled. "If it'd make you feel better, mister, just hold a gun in your hand."

The second one, however, was curious.

"Let him git it, Dolf."

"I never said he couldn't, did I? Go ahead. Only move sorta slowlike."

Shamrock, watching them both, looped the reins over his arm, unbuttoned his shirt, and untied the knot in the two bandannas. He pulled them out and held them up.

"Shall I throw it?"

"To me," the shorter one said.

Shamrock threw it, and the man caught it easily. While he was unwrapping it, eyes on Shamrock, Shamrock pulled the bay around so it quarter-faced them. The second guard smiled at the movement, but did not move his hands from his belt.

Even when his companion cursed, this man did not take his gaze from Shamrock.

"The cell keys, by God!"

"Uh-huh," Shamrock said, hunching forward a little. "Now give 'em back," he taunted. "You won't need 'em."

But he was watching the first speaker, not watching his eyes but the upper part of the forearm. And when Shamrock saw the shirt sleeve move, he acted, streaking his gun up in a tight outward-flipping arc that exploded waist-high even as he was rolling out of the saddle. He landed on his shoulder just as a shot slammed and the bay reared. Shamrock rolled clear over onto one knee, gun in hand.

"Look out!" Maginnis yelled, and he yanked his horse straight over into the second man's.

Shamrock paused, noting without seeing that the other guard, the silent one, had folded onto his saddle horn. The bay had gone down now.

The guard on the other side of Maginnis shot again, just after Maginnis's horse slammed into him, and missed.

Shamrock's second shot was low, blind, and it hit Maginnis's sorrel. The horse screamed, folded down on one knee as Maginnis pitched forward, leaving the upper half of the guard's body clear.

Shamrock opened up, emptying his gun in one chattering blast that was hardly a second long.

Then he rose. The guard tried to say something, scream something, as he was slammed out of his saddle. When he hit the ground, Shamrock raced to Maginnis.

The sorrel was on his side, kicking, Maginnis pinned under him, terror in his eyes.

Shamrock loaded his gun and shot the sorrel, and after a last conclusive kick, the horse settled quietly on its side.

"You hurt, kid?"

Maginnis shook his head.

Without even looking at the two guards, Shamrock drew his knife and cut the hobbles under the horse's belly, which freed Maginnis's legs.

"Can you work out?"

Again Maginnis shook his head.

The sorrel was lying almost in the center of the arroyo, his feet against the curve of the four-inch bank. Shamrock went over to the roan, who had stood utterly still through it all. His rider, the tall guard, had piled onto the ground, face first, and lay there, his hands doubled up under his chest, his Stetson still on.

Shamrock took the rope from the saddle and went over to Maginnis. Then he squatted in front of the sorrel's belly.

"Can you stick it out, kid? It hurts, don't it?"

"It's numb," Maginnis said, and smiled. "It don't hurt a-tall."

"Hold tight a minute."

Shamrock worked out a loop in the rope, then raised the sorrel's head and slipped the loop over it. He worked the loop back until it was against the shoulders, then he built it bigger and slipped it under the sorrel's front legs and pulled it as tight as he could.

Then he led the roan over close, dallied the rope on the horn, mounted, and started the roan. It tightened the loop just behind the sorrel's shoulder.

"I'm goin' to pull, kid. I won't skid him off you, but I'll pull slow. He's got his feet against the bank and he ought to raise a little before he skids. When he does, you kite out. Can you do it?"

"Sure," Maginnis said.

Shamrock eased the roan into the load. The sorrel wasn't big, but the roan's footing was uphill and it was work. Shamrock talked to him, urged him, roweled him mildly, and the roan put his weight into it. Shamrock felt the rope tighten, go taut, then he felt the roan making progress by inches. He looked back, and Maginnis was fighting wildly to pull his leg out. The roan moved ahead six inches, and Maginnis broke free, just as the roan was pulled back.

Shamrock dismounted and walked over to the kid. He was standing now, testing his leg gingerly.

"It ain't broke," he said, grinning up into Shamrock's face.

Shamrock smiled back, his face thawing into a real grin of pleasure. "You aren't as salty as you were in jail," he said. "Not by half."

"I thought you was one of 'em," Maginnis replied sturdily. "You—you ain't, are you?"

"No," Shamrock said simply. "Do you believe that?"

Maginnis nodded.

"Let's look at that leg."

Examination revealed only a raw, livid bruise on Maginnis's thigh and calf, where the horse had fallen on him. The soft sand had saved him from a broken leg.

Assured, Shamrock walked over to the body of the smaller guard. His left hand still clutched the red bandannas as he lay on his back staring at the sky. The other guard had a single mark, a clean hole almost in the middle of his chest. He had never known what hit him. Shamrock looked up to find Maginnis watching him.

The youngster gulped. "Them devils!" he said passionately. "I reckon you saved my life."

"Huh-uh. You saved your own—and mine—by pullin' your horse into that other jasper's."

The kid was about to protest when Shamrock silenced him. "You go gather in that paint"—he pointed to the smaller guard's horse, which had been stampeded by the fight and was now standing a dozen yards off, reins trailing—"and throw my saddle on that roan."

It was useless to try to hide the bodies of the two guards, but Shamrock didn't want the buzzards to pick them. It was quick work to haul them clear of the arroyo and pile rocks on them where Lobell could see it. Not that he would have any doubts when Harmer got to him with his story. He hurried through the business, hating it on account of Maginnis. Fifteen years old was a little too young to see things like this.

Finished, he walked back to Maginnis, who was standing grim-faced by the paint.

"Let's get off the trail," Shamrock suggested. "And while we're at it, we might try to cover up our tracks."

He mounted and picked his way carefully, sticking to the rock and larger gravel that would make tracking difficult. He headed for the mesa and traveled its level length until they reached the end of it. From here they could see the hills that hid the town and the road leading from it.

Shamrock dismounted and lay down in the shade of a cedar. Maginnis, limping a little, did likewise.

Shamrock rolled a cigarette and lighted it, not speaking for a while. The sun was scarce an hour from setting, and the air was beginning to dissolve into the evening translucence it has in the dry country. The hushed, waiting east stretched before them, almost to infinity. Far off in New Mexico, low mountains lifted their blue *sierras* scarcely higher than the light-green sky of the horizon rim. Closer, the country slanted off into red flats, to fawn-colored dry lands, to purple hills whose every angle was etched in black, and finally to blue of crawling space that had no dimension of perspective. It lay sprawled under the cobalt monotone of the sky, huge, ungrasped, so limitless it exhausted the eye.

Maginnis was watching it, too, his face working strangely. He wiped his eyes with his sleeve, but Shamrock kept utterly still.

"I reckon I'm just a—"

"Forget it," Shamrock said gently. "If it's been ballin' up inside you, why not?"

Maginnis grinned shyly. "Got the makin's?" he asked

gruffly.

Shamrock handed him his Durham sack and did not laugh at the fat inch of cigarette Maginnis built, nor at the cough it brought. Slowly, in that wordless communion, Maginnis's face lost its tautness.

"I wisht I had a gun," he said suddenly.

"I thought you would. That's why I took one off that towhead. It's in that slicker on the roan's saddle."

"Thanks," Maginnis said huskily.

"Might's well start from the beginnin'," Shamrock said presently. "Even to the name."

"It's Lee," Maginnis began. "Same as my old man. He died in this country, not far from here, when I wasn't more than fourteen or so."

"That couldn't have been more than a couple of years ago," Shamrock said after a moment's thought.

"No. He died in town."

"In Malpais Springs?"

Maginnis nodded and said tonelessly, "Not town exactly. Just on the edge. He died swingin' from that big cottonwood just across the bridge."

"No," Shamrock said softly.

Maginnis nodded. "Lynched. Lynched for killin' that old devil of a Hyatt."

"Mayo's father?"

"Yes." He looked at Shamrock. "But he never done it, though. I know Dad. I'd seen him when he was murderin'-mad, and I know. Nothin' in the world would've made him kill a man—except someone he caught beatin' a horse or cheatin' at cards, maybe."

"Go on," Shamrock said, cursing himself because he had not thought to question Hyatt when he mentioned his father's death.

Maginnis thought a minute. "Dad was prospectin'—always had. He wanted me raised with a family and women-folks, so he put me with an aunt down in Tucson. He wrote reg'lar. He kinda liked me, and I reckon I was that way about him. We'd made big plans for as soon as I was growed up. Then one day word come to my aunt that Dad had killed a rancher named Hyatt up in this country, and that he'd been lynched for it—took out of jail and strung up."

"Lobell's jail?"

"His jail," Maginnis said grimly. He went on: "That was about a year after it happened that the news came. They tried to keep me there in Tucson, but I run away. I kept workin' up to this country, sometimes swampin' long enough for stage fare to the next town, sometimes workin' in stables. Everyone I talked to, I asked about this lynchin' —and about Lobell. By the time I hit here a couple of months ago, I knew enough to know that if I wanted to stay in town, I'd better change my name. I did—to McKinley." He smiled at Shamrock. "You know I never thought I'd told you I was Maginnis till after you'd gone, then I thought you'd never think about it."

"I'm sorry I ever did," Shamrock said. "Go on."

"I got one letter from Dad before he died, mailed less than a week before the lynchin'." He scowled and looked down at his heels. "I memorized it. Here's the way it went: " 'Son—I've got holt of somethin' big. If I get the backin' I need and got to have, we'll buy us so many horses you'll be an old man before you've rid 'em all once. More later. Love, Dad.' "

Shamrock whistled softly. "Gold, then."

"Couldn't be anything else, could it?" Maginnis asked gravely, as though questioning an elder.

Shamrock didn't answer. He was thinking of something else, of the elder Hyatt, Nancy's and Mayo's father.

"Your dad ever have any trouble with Hyatt?"

"A little. Hyatt and a Double Diamond rider caught

Dad fillin' his burro kegs at a lake up in the Ritas that sets on Double Diamond land. He ordered Dad off and Dad went, after tellin' him that he'd never denied a dog water and he never thought he'd live to see the day when a dog would deny him water, but he had."

"Did your dad write that?" Shamrock asked quickly.

"No. I got that from the Double Diamond rider. He's gone now."

"How was Hyatt killed?"

"Ambushed. They found the tracks of a burro and a prospector's hand pick with Dad's initials burned on it near the body." He looked up at Shamrock. "It was a fresh burn. Dad never marked his stuff. Why would he when he traveled by himself?"

"Where was he when Lobell got him?"

"In town. Lobell arrested him and took him to jail. Then the talk started—wrong talk, about how Dad had insulted Nancy Hyatt and old man Hyatt ordered him off the place. And—and other things. None of it was true. Then the mob started. Lobell made out like he was fightin' 'em off, but a bunch of 'em got him and tied him up and took Dad out across the bridge."

Shamrock looked off into the east, watching the sun magnify and clarify every ridge and gut and break in the land until it looked painted on a flat canvas.

"That ain't all," Maginnis said softly. "I've talked as much as I could—pretendin' dumb, askin' questions—and I reckon I've got a good hunch who started the lynchin' talk."

"I think I know," Shamrock said, "but tell me."

For answer, Maginnis pointed a bony arm in the direction from which they had come. "They're buried over there—two of 'em. But not all. You've seen some of the others."

Shamrock nodded wearily. It was the old story, greed

and murder masquerading behind the might of the law. But had old Maginnis gone to the sheriff with the story and location of his gold and Lobell killed him to get it? Shamrock doubted it, for most of these old prospectors were tight-lipped and distrustful of their fellow men. A man didn't leave the secret of a fortune with any chance acquaintance. But who had Maginnis told? The man or men that were backing him.

And who were they?

"You've never stumbled on to the backer your dad mentioned?" he asked Maginnis.

"Never a trace."

Yet they must be close, Shamrock reflected, for old Maginnis had been staying in Malpais Springs when Lobell arrested him.

"You wrote the claim office if he had anything registered?"

Maginnis nodded. "He had fifty, but none of them were near here—not anywhere near."

That was understandable, too, for registry would give away the location of his claim and start a rush. Old Maginnis had been smart enough to try and make a dicker with a rich backer who could form a company. He could name his own price, and then with the capital behind him, could go to the spot and sew it up—all of it, every foot of it. And there the trail blanked out—blanked by old Maginnis's horse-trading sense and his caution.

"Lobell knows," Maginnis said, his voice cold with hate. "He knows who paid him to throw the blame for the Hyatt killin' on Dad. If he don't know where Dad's claim was, he knows who does know. Damn him!" he said passionately. "All hell won't hold the outlaw I'm goin' to turn into."

"They ain't all like him, Lee," Shamrock said truthfully. "There are good sheriffs, and when they're good, men don't come better. Don't let a crook like Lobell toll you into the biggest mistake a man can make."

Maginnis studied him silently, then said with surprising candor, "You're on the dodge, ain't you?"

Shamrock nodded and rose wearily. "That's why I know what I'm talkin' about."

"All right," Maginnis said, a little reluctantly. "But I'm goin' to get good with a gun."

Shamrock smiled a little. "Good. And I'm goin' to send you to a man that can teach you."

A shadow of fear flitted across Maginnis's face. "Who?"

"Mayo Hyatt."

"That killer?" Maginnis cried. "He'd gun me in a second, just like Lobell would."

"Why?"

"Why, my dad killed his, he thinks."

"Maybe all dads weren't like yours," Shamrock said. "Ole man Hyatt drove Mayo to the Wild Bunch. Mayo never liked him. You go to him with this same story. God knows you should have done it before, but you didn't know that. He'll do to ride the river with."

Maginnis looked doubtful.

"I mean it."

"If you say so, it's so," Maginnis said.

Shamrock told him of the camp at the Notch, and persuaded him that there lay his greatest safety.

"Where you goin'?"

"I'll be around."

"But where?"

"In town. I'm a deputy," Shamrock said dryly.

"He'll get you."

"He hasn't yet," Shamrock said, a little grimly. "Now high-tail it. You'll be with friends."

Maginnis nodded solemnly, and Shamrock gave him the gun from the slicker. The youngster strapped it on. On his lean shank it hung big as a smoked ham. When he straightened up, his face was grave, but strangely untroubled.

"Now high-tail it," Shamrock said.

Maginnis mounted the paint and looked at Shamrock.

"So long, partner. Take care of yourself," he said simply, and waved an arm.

"So long, partner."

CHAPTER ELEVEN

Shamrock loafed on the way back to town, loafed till way past dark. Carefully, tenaciously, he thought over what Maginnis had told him. Now, at long last, he began to see Lobell's game. If the sheriff could hang a killing on an innocent man, why not go a step farther and say that Lobell himself killed the elder Hyatt? Why? To get the Double Diamond, or make the way clear for ruining it by sending his half-dozen gunmen to rustle it clean. But the ranch was going to the bank, and if Lobell wanted it, he would have to get it from the bank. Ah, but what if the bank wanted it, too? What if it had hired Lobell to get it for them? All right, there was one theory, but a pretty obvious one. He segregated that theory: the bank wanted Hyatt's ranch.

Now about the elder Maginnis. He wanted backing for his mine. Where did men go who wanted financial backing for their affairs? More often than not to a bank. All right, say Maginnis had gone to the bank for his financial backing, and had told them of his gold. Then the bank stood to profit most by old Maginnis's death, didn't it? Could they have been interested in the lynching?

If so, that left the bank convicted of murder on two

counts, Hyatt's and Maginnis's.

Then Shamrock considered the other side:

A bank is in business for the dinero. It foreclosed on the Double Diamond as a bad risk. It sent its papers through the law and Lobell. *As for the bank backin' Maginnis, how do I know? And that,* he concluded, *leaves me just where I was.*

But it didn't, either. Why had the bank picked on Hyatt and the Double Diamond? In a prosperous cattle country, didn't almost every rancher borrow money from the bank, and put his spread in the same position as Hyatt had the Double Diamond? Of course. Then could it be that the Double Diamond was a better ranch, more desirable than the others?

Shamrock didn't know, but he knew where he could find out. He knew, too, that he was going to see the banker, size him up, question him if he could. He would be safe from Lobell until Harmer was free.

He entered town the same way he left it and rode straight to the courthouse. There was no light there, but he was careful in his approach. The door was open, the corridor dark.

Pinckney's door was still locked, and the place looked as if no one had been there.

He unlocked the door, paused inside the room, and listened, but nothing disturbed the silence. He struck a match, found a lamp and lighted it, then unlocked the big padlock and swung open the door.

Pinckney and Harmer were sitting in the dark, and they squinted up at him in sullen anger.

"Come out of there, Pinckney," Shamrock said, motioning with his gun.

Both got up, but Shamrock leveled his Colt. "Stay there, Harmer. You, Pinckney. Get me a land plat of the county—Jicarilla County."

Pinckney returned to his prison and presently emerged with a big map, which Shamrock took.

"Look here. How long are you going to keep us here?"

"I dunno yet. Get back in there."

He locked the door again, then sat down at the desk and spread out the map and studied it. Slowly, by bits, it told its story.

Jicarilla County was a big one, Western-fashion, and was roughly square. A good bit of it was made up of the Santa Ritas, the rest of it the foothills of the eastern slope. Shamrock laboriously interpreted the contour lines, and concluded that the west slope of the Ritas was entirely on end, canyon-shot, steep, and judging from the complete absence of sizable creeks and streams, dry as a bone. He found the Notch Hyatt had mentioned and noted with some surprise that it was very deep, almost a thousand feet lower than the surrounding peaks. Below it on the eastern slope lay a small lake, doubtless the one Hyatt had forbidden old Maginnis to use.

Finished, he got up and unlocked the door again, gun in hand.

"Can we go?" Pinkney asked.

"No. I want a list of all the Double Diamond holdin's—every foot of land they ever held."

"We haven't got it."

Shamrock regarded him coldly. "Have I got to beat it out of you?"

"I say we haven't got it."

"You lie," Shamrock said calmly. "You'd have to have it for taxes. Maybe you'd like to sit in there until you remember where it is."

Pinckney, cursing, went back into the depths of the room and emerged presently with a paper.

"Come out here," Shamrock said. "I want you to read them off to me."

Pinckney stepped out, and Shamrock locked the door on Harmer again.

He seated Pinckney across the desk, looking first in all the drawers for a gun and finding none.

Then, the map spread before them, gun in one hand trained on Pinckney, pencil in the other hand, he sat down.

He pointed the gun straight at Pinckney across the desk. "Make a move and I'll let this off. I won't even look up. Now start readin'."

Section by section, Pinckney read off the Hyatt holdings, and Shamrock noted them on the map. It was slow, tedious, but gradually Shamrock built up a picture of the Double Diamond domain. By lease or purchase, it amounted to more than three townships—over seventy thousand acres of prime grazing land. And a good bit of it, Shamrock noted, lay along the feeder creeks to the lake, and along the outlet creek of the lake clear down onto the flats. This, according to Pinckney, was outright purchase and was bought first and held to date. Old Hyatt had been smart enough to get his water first, then, with it certain, he had spread out.

Shamrock got a good picture of the elder Hyatt. He was a gambler who had seen a chance to carve out a cattle kingdom in the Ritas. He must have had to borrow heavily to satisfy his appetite for land. Perhaps if he had lived, he would have swung it, but it had crumbled now. And doing it he had doubtless made many enemies.

Shamrock leaned back, frowning.

"Is the Double Diamond the biggest spread around here?"

"There's a coupl_ bigger—maybe better, too. I dunno."

"Whose?"

"Scott's Tumblin S over south and Carney's Pine Tree brand way north."

112

"Did they get on with old man Hyatt?"

Pinckney surveyed him shrewdly a moment, then said, "They did not. Hyatt drove a hard bargain with anyone he had dealin's with."

Shamrock rose, and Pinckney with him.

"You goin' to turn us loose now?" he asked.

"So you can go to Lobell?" Shamrock asked, and laughed briefly. "Hardly. I'll come let you out later. Get back in the cage, mister."

Pinckney cursed him bitterly, but Shamrock was deaf to both his pleas and his oaths. He opened the door and herded Pinckney in with Harmer again.

"Whose horse was that bay out in the corral?" he asked.

"Mine."

"What's he worth, saddle and all?"

"Seventy-five dollars," Pinckney said immediately. The horse was worthy thirty, the saddle twenty, so Shamrock counted out fifty dollars and threw them on the floor.

Harmer was watching, and when the bay was mentioned, he looked suspiciously at Shamrock.

Shamrock laughed at him. "Why'd I buy it, Harmer?"

"I dunno," Harmer said sullenly.

"Think a minute," Shamrock jeered. "He's dead. I'll tell you that much."

And he slammed the door in their faces.

Outside, he freed the roan he had taken from the gunman, looped the reins over his head, and let him stand. Eventually, Lobell would find him.

Then he turned toward town. He had learned something from Pinckney, anyway. There was no obvious reason why the bank—if it was the bank—should have been so set on getting the Double Diamond. It was big, but other spreads were bigger.

He walked past the sheriff's office and saw Freed sitting there. Lobell was gone. Where? He would have asked

Freed, but he did not want anyone to know his where-abouts.

But he had to know where Lobell was, for he intended to see the banker, and if Lobell walked in on him, it would be hard to explain.

He crossed the street to the Legal Tender, and stepped inside the doors. Lobell wasn't there.

Outside again, he headed up the street, looking up and down the sidewalks that were lighted by the lamps from the stores. Should he go back and ask Freed?

Then, up the street, just stepping out of a doorway, he saw the familiar bulk of the sheriff, who turned and started toward him.

Shamrock stepped quickly into the first doorway handy and looked around him. It was a saddle shop.

He entered, walked the length of it until he was in the midst of a tangle of gear strewn over the back end.

An aproned old man, dry and tough as the leather he worked, sat at a bench.

Shamrock nodded to him and sat down on a saddle, hidden from sight of the street. Rolling a cigarette, he looked around him, observing two new saddles up for display on a rough sawhorse. They were sturdy-looking with the right depth of swell, the round skirt, the sparseness of stamping that Shamrock liked.

"Sell many?" he asked pleasantly.

The old man was stretching and tacking wet hide over the beechwood tree of the saddle, and when he looked up his hands went on working by feel. Behind his thick glasses, his eyes were bright and dark, and his thin hair was pearly white and clean.

"Not many," he said, his tone friendly. "They cost too much. But I have a lot of 'em come in and look." He laughed, Shamrock with him.

"I'm lookin' for the banker," Shamrock said, after a

moment's silence. "Where can I find him?"

"The hotel."

"Hotel?"

"Sure. He owns it, and he's so damned tight he sets up nights figgerin' ways to cheat hisself out of the room rent," the old man said with mild bitterness.

"What's his name?"

"Gillespie. Jacob Courtland Gillespie."

Shamrock smiled. "What's he ever done to you?"

The old man nodded to include the room. "There was a time, son, when I used this here room for storin' my trade-ins. I spread out a little too much—or too fast, I dunno which." He shrugged. "The bank took over my shop ten years ago."

"Gillespie?"

The old man nodded. "I'd of made it, but I needed time. I thought I had it, but it wasn't in writin'. So he got it."

"He don't seem much of a favorite around here," Shamrock hazarded.

"He ain't—not since the day he trimmed up a horse out on the street with an ax handle." He chuckled. "He got knocked clean over the hitchrack onto the sidewalk. But, hell, I reckon he ain't no different than any banker, though. They live on a man's hard luck. Ain't that so?"

"Some of 'em," Shamrock agreed, rising. "Some's all right. Some's pretty mean, too."

At the door he was just in time to see Lobell step into the sheriff's office. He looked across the street and up it several doors to where the bank stood. It was a brick building, the only one in town, and had the raw, angular ugliness peculiar to its kind. It was the first time he had noticed it, and he studied it with a wondering distaste.

Then he stepped into the street and crossed to the hotel. The clerk was not at the desk. Shamrock heard a pounding out in the back room and walked through the musty lobby to the dining-room, the back of which looked out on the alley. The old clerk was kneeling on the floor by a window.

When he looked up at Shamrock's approach, his face was fretted. He was in the act of replacing a broken pane in the window by the uncertain light of a lamp on a near-by table.

"Look at that!" he said sourly, pointing to the paneless window. "Every time one of them bat-eared cowpokes buys a rope from Sanders, he stretches it for 'em on that big post he has for shed support. When they get through, what do you reckon they do?"

"What?"

"They ride back out the alley past the hotel here, and they're usually tryin' the rope to see if it's limber. They flick it at one of these windows here, and, by hell, they break one every time. They know danged well it takes a year to git glass up here and half the time it's busted when it gits here, but do they think of that? Hell, no. They hightail it out the alley before I can see who they are."

"Where's Gillespie's room?" Shamrock asked.

"Mr. Gillespie?" the clerk said, immediately respectful, and Shamrock nodded. "Third floor. The stairs is at the last door to your left on the second-floor corridor. It ain't really the third floor," he explained. "His room's the only one there. You won't have no trouble findin' it. You just—"

Shamrock cut him short. "Is he in?"

"I reckon. He ain't been down to supper yet, though. You must go—"

But Shamrock fled before the old man's garrulity. On the second floor he found the door opening onto a steep stair. Gillespie's room must be right under the rafters, he reflected as he struck a match and stumbled up the steps. He had no idea what he was going to say to Gillespie, except to ask him questions about the Double Diamond until Gillespie lost his temper and ordered him out.

The door was immediately to the left at the top of the stairs. Shamrock knocked. There was no answer. He knocked again, long and loud, but still he got no answer.

Maybe Gillespie was asleep. Shamrock tried the knob and found the door unlocked, so he opened it and stepped into the room. It was dark, but there was the warm smell of a lamp recently blown out—that, and another smell less pleasant. A window, low to the right, was cut in the roof slope.

Shamrock struck a match and looked around.

He sucked his breath in sharply and dropped the match.

"God!" he said softly, sharply, fumbling for another match.

When he had struck it, he walked slowly over to the lone armchair by the bed.

A man was tied in it, gagged. There was a neat bullet hole in his forehead that had not trickled blood. On the pinched, rather narrow face, there was a look of arrested horror that made Shamrock's hackles rise. The man wore a rusty suit of black, a soft shirt, and a string tie.

His boots and socks had been pulled off, and his feet tied together. With a rising gorge, Shamrock saw that his feet had been horribly burned, and the faint odor of seared flesh still hung about him.

"Tortured and killed," Shamrock muttered, as the match died.

He was about to strike another when he heard a step on the stair.

CHAPTER TWELVE

"MR. GILLESPIE!" a woman's voice called up the stairway.

Shamrock held his breath. Then the woman began the ascent. Doubtless it was one of the hotel help calling Gillespie to supper. Shamrock knew he could prove an alibi since he had talked to the clerk not two minutes before, yet he did not want the sheriff to know he had come to talk with Gillespie.

He eased the door shut and made for the window. It was already open. He crawled out onto the sloping roof and could see the dark blot of the next building's roof below.

It wouldn't be much of a drop. He let go the sill and started to slide, feet first. When he hit the roof edge, he was going fast and he sailed off it to drop the six feet to the roof of the adjoining building. It sloped the opposite way, so immediately he started to slide again.

Luckily, the buildings were close together, and Shamrock broke his descent just at the gutter trough by putting out his feet against the side of the hotel. It took only a few seconds to work his way to the alley end of the building and to swing down to the alley.

Even as he hit the ground, he dimly heard a woman's scream. He swung in the back door of the hotel, which opened onto a corridor running straight through.

There was no one in the lobby, and he sat down in a chair.

He was sitting there when the woman screamed again from the top of the main stairs.

"Mr. Gillespie! He's been killed! Murdered!"

Shamrock took the stairs two at a time, and got her story.

"I'll get the sheriff," he said.

At the dining-room door he called the clerk, who was already halfway across the room, and told him the news.

Then he stepped out onto the sidewalk and turned to the sheriff's office. Whoever had done the killing had escaped the same way he did, Shamrock knew. It was done after dark. Gillespie had been tortured. For what?

Lobell was visiting with a stranger when Shamrock entered.

"Gillespie has been murdered," Shamrock announced. In his explanation on the way back to the hotel, he was careful to tell the sheriff how he happened to be the bearer of the tidings.

The sheriff, grim and silent, listened and said nothing, only occasionally clucking his tongue.

In the banker's room, they found the clerk, white and trembling. He had touched nothing.

The room was a mean place, Shamrock saw now, with a cot for a bed, a deal table, two chairs, a wardrobe, and a lamp, with the roof slope for a ceiling. In the far corner was a small heating stove.

The sheriff surveyed Gillespie in silence.

"Tortured, huh?" he said to Shamrock.

Lobell looked around the room and walked over to the stove and laid his hand on it. He jerked it away quickly. Seeing a poker lying at the edge of the woodbox, he picked it up, looked at it, then smelled it. He put it down in disgust.

"That's what they used, by God."

Going over to Gillespie, he shook his head slowly.

"Goddlemighty. Gag a man before they torture him so he can't cry out." He looked up at Shamrock. "Why? What'd they want?"

"He's a banker," Shamrock said.

Still the sheriff looked at him, as if trying to puzzle out the meaning of the statement. Then his face lit up. "Oh. Money?"

"See if he's got his keys," Shamrock said.

Lobell searched Gillespie and found nothing except some pencils, some dog-eared letters and a wallet with money in it.

"He ain't been robbed," Lobell said.

"No," Shamrock said impatiently. "He hasn't got any keys, either. Why would they take beer money when they got a whole bank to work on?"

"Ah," Lobell said softly. "That's it. They'd git in the bank with them keys—but everything's in the vault."

"Why do you think they tortured him?" Shamrock asked patiently.

Lobell looked at him blankly, then as the meaning came to him, his eyes narrowed. "Uh-huh. Uh-huh. I see. Come on."

He paused just long enough to warn the clerk not to touch a thing and go for the coroner. Then they went downstairs and four doors down to the bank building. The front door was firmly locked.

"Try the back," Shamrock suggested.

"Hell, he wouldn't carry a key for that," Lobell growled, but they went around and tried it. It was open.

Lobell struck a match, walked in, and looked around.

Freed and three or four curious men, strangers to Shamrock, stepped through the door behind them.

The match died, but Lobell had already spotted a lamp on a desk behind the railing that separated the customers from the business space.

Up front there was a separate glassed-in office, marked *Private*. The rear third of the room, except for the narrow passageway to the back door, was the vault.

Lobell picked up the lamp and held it over his head.

The vault door was open.

"You're right, by God!" he said grimly. Several other men had begun to ease in through the back door, for apparently the news had spread fast. Lobell's fat gunman—Harmer's friend—was among them.

"I don't mind you men in here," Lobell said to them, "but don't disturb nothin'. Don't come in the vault."

He walked into the vault, Shamrock behind him, Freed and the other deputy behind Shamrock, and the half-dozen others behind them.

The floor of the vault was littered with papers, and the strong boxes on the shelves were awry, but not opened. The big cash box that sat on the top of an old and unused safe was open.

"Gone," Lobell said, pointing to it. "I've seen him put the cash in that there thing when he locks up at night." He looked at his deputies. "Cleaned out."

The watchers all looked at each other and said nothing. Lobell swore bitterly as he set the lamp down on the safe.

"Just don't move much," he instructed, "and we'll look around here."

He started picking up the papers off the floor, looking at each as he did so. The deputies, including Shamrock, did the same.

Suddenly Freed made a noise in his throat, and pointed to an object lying under a paper on the floor.

"What is it?" Lobell said.

"Gillespie's keys, I reckon."

He picked them up and gave them to Lobell.

Lobell took one look at them, then his jaw clicked shut with a snap. He rose, folded the keys in his hand, and addressed the men in the doorway.

"I'm goin' to show you these. See if you recognize them," he told them. "Don't say nothin' until everyone's seen it."

Then he unfolded his fist and held the keys in his palm as he walked over to the door.

The key ring was a strong gold chain. A hole had been drilled in a huge, polished elk's tooth and the chain threaded through it and clasped. Years of being carried in a pocket had polished the tooth until it glistened like some malformed pearl. Four or five keys were on the chain.

The first man glanced at it perfunctorily, then passed it to his companion. It went the rounds, none of them looking at it more than a half second.

When it was handed back to Lobell, he said, "It ain't Gillespie's, is it?"

The men shook their heads.

"Whose is it?"

"Dick Hyatt's," one said bluntly.

"Hyatt's old man."

"Hyatt—old man Hyatt."

The replies were unanimous.

"You sure you ain't mistaken?" the sheriff said.

"Hell, no," one man replied. "I know the man that was on the huntin' trip up in Wyomin' with Dick Hyatt when he shot the elk that tooth come from."

"Uh-huh. That's what I thought," Lobell said.

He looked at the men in silence. No one spoke for a long moment, then one of the watchers—a man of Lobell's age with the rough, weathered features of a rancher—said, "Hell, Lobell. Speak it out. That damned redheaded gunman son of his did it!"

"Lost his ranch to the bank and aimed to git even with Gillespie," another supplemented angrily. "That's a mite too raw even for that killer to git away with."

"He won't," the old rancher said grimly, and turned away to go.

"Wait, Gill!" Lobell ordered.

The old rancher stopped.

"I know what you aim to do," the sheriff said, "but I'm warnin' you right now. If you raise a bunch of them saloon bums for a posse, I'm goin' to arm Hyatt and we'll fight you till we're all killed off."

Gill glared at him. "What's the difference? It comes out the same."

"No, it don't," Lobell said sternly, "not anywhere near. You git good steady men—men you can trust that won't lose their heads. If we catch him, we're goin' to bring him back here and he's goin' to stand trial in front of Judge Thomson—not Judge Lynch. I think I can find him, and he'll likely put up a fight. But I'm goin' up there with only a couple of my deputies and take the chance of losin' him rather than take a bunch of drunk cowpokes along to work off a grudge on a lynchin' spree."

"All right," Gill said. He knew as well as Lobell did that the mob would do whatever suited it, and when he left, he was smiling to himself.

Shamrock had been watching quietly. When the keys were finally identified, he could scarcely believe the evidence. Had Hyatt, fed up with this endless persecution, finally turned on his tormentors? Shamrock couldn't believe it. Neither could he believe that Hyatt would torture a man as Gillespie had been tortured. Yet the evidence pointed to Hyatt. It could, of course, be planted evidence, but if so, who had planted it and who had killed Gillespie and robbed the bank? Lobell? That seemed unlikely since Lobell and Gillespie were working together. Nevertheless, Lobell was ready to blame Hyatt and to lynch him.

Moreover, Lobell was not lying when he said he could find Hyatt. All he would have had to do was to put a man to watch the Double Diamond and see where Hyatt went.

Shamrock turned a little pale with the fury bottled up in him. His knuckles went white from clenching his fists, but his face was cold, impassive.

The sheriff turned to his deputies. "Well, I reckon that's all." He sighed. "It's a nasty job all around."

For a moment he looked at Shamrock. Maybe it was something Shamrock imagined, or maybe it was some inner exultation at the perfection of his scheme to get Hyatt, but Lobell's eyes for an instant were those of a madman's— a man drunk with hate and power and success. Then he smiled a little at Shamrock, as if to say, "You know. I think you know, anyway. If you do, make the most of it."

"Let's go," he said.

Shamrock appeared to be in no particular hurry, waiting while the sheriff blew out the light and locked the door. But all the time, he was casting about desperately for a way to break away. Hyatt—and Maginnis, too—had to be warned, or as surely as they were alive now, they would be dead before morning, both of them.

There was nothing more now that Shamrock could learn about Lobell, and nothing he could learn from Gillespie. That was sealed for eternity, thanks perhaps to Lobell. There was no reason for staying longer with the sheriff. But if he wanted to get out alive, he would have to be careful.

Lobell and his deputies were joined by a group of curious men at the back door, and they made their way down the alley toward the sheriff's office.

"I'm goin' to get some shells," Shamrock said, and before Lobell could stop him he broke away and entered the back door of Sanders's store. The plump deputy—George, Lobell had called him—like a patient dog, was at his heels.

Inside the store, Shamrock glared at him truculently.

"I'm goin' to get some, too," George said.

Waiting for the shells, Shamrock knew it would be suicide to try to break away now. Blue was still at the hitchrack in front of the sheriff's office. He would never make it there before the alarm was given, and pursuit started.

And the sheriff, once sure of Shamrock's intent, would hunt him down like a mad dog.

He received the shells and stepped out the back door again, George by his side.

Lobell and the crowd were in the office, and Shamrock could see the sheriff passing out guns. Blue, patient in hip-shot somnolence, was at the rack.

Crossing the road toward Blue, Shamrock decided to chance it. There was a moderate crowd on the streets, which would delay the sheriff's pursuit.

He let his hand drop to his side as they came in behind Blue. Suddenly he blurred up his Colt as he pivoted and rammed it into George's belly.

"I dare you to yell," he said quietly. "Don't put up your hands!"

George's slack, idiot face hardly changed, and he said nothing. Shamrock reached out, flipped his gun from its holster, then kicked it under the heels of a near-by horse.

A man passing on the sidewalk in front of the sheriff's office looked at them, but Shamrock's back was turned to the walk, so that his body shielded his gun and made it appear as if the two of them were in conversation.

When the man passed, Shamrock said, "I'm leavin', but I'll be back. Tell Lobell that, will you?"

"I'll tell him," George said, his loose lips twisted in a derisive grin. "He might even hunt you out."

"He won't have to," Shamrock said flatly. "I'll be back on my own. There's a couple of things I got to say to him yet, but they can wait." He reached in his pocket and drew out the courthouse keys. "Go down and let that pardner of yours out. He's locked up in Pinckney's vault."

He backed off to Blue, untied the reins, looped them over Blue's head, all the while covering George.

Suddenly a voice spoke from the steps of the sheriff's office.

"Who's that with the gun, George?"

Shamrock whirled to see a man on the steps in the act of drawing his gun. Shamrock flipped a shot at him, drove him back into the office half doubled up, then vaulted onto Blue.

George, unmindful of the horses, had dived for his gun underneath their hoofs. Shamrock leaned far out of the saddle and brought his gun down viciously on George's head, just as the fat hand closed on the gun.

Then he swung out into the road, leaning low over Blue's neck. He crossed the four corners at a gallop, scattering pedestrians to either side as he made for the bridge. A fusillade of shots ripped into the night behind him, but they were high on account of the crowd.

Blue's hoofs made thunder on the bridge as Shamrock reached the other side. It was a head start, anyway.

CHAPTER THIRTEEN

For the way to the Notch, the map at the courthouse and Hyatt's vague instructions were all Shamrock had to go by. At the top of the hill across from town, he pulled off the road and headed straight northwest.

He remembered from the map that the lake lay just below the Notch, and that the outlet creek flowed almost in a straight line east and a little south until it reached the flats. If he picked up the creek, he could reach the lake and the Notch.

He cursed bitterly. It would be slow work, and each minute counted, but he had no choice. Cutting straight for the foothills, he had ridden half an hour when he crossed a stream. He followed it, only to find that it turned south after two miles. He gave it up, cursing, and headed north and west again.

Blue found the second creek and drank deeply. Then Shamrock followed it through the foothills, up, up, wading it part of the time, threading the narrow canyons it had cut, swerving away from it when the going got too rough, but always keeping a course not far from it. Blue worked doggedly.

For three hours Shamrock rode only by the light of the stars, fighting his impatience—and his gathering fear. For Lobell knew the country, and would kill his horse taking the most direct route. Somewhere up near the Notch, Hyatt, Nancy, Matt, and Maginnis would be sitting around a campfire, while all hell was riding for them.

When he was getting desperate, wondering if he was following the wrong creek, the country leveled off and he smelled the cold wetness of water.

The timber was thick and deep and dark where he had been traveling the creek, but now it broke away. Shortly he came to a lake nestled in a natural basin surrounded by great Navajo pines and aspens. It was a big lake, as far as he could make out, and its size surprised him.

He skirted it and took his direction by the stars, heading straight west. Beyond, higher still, lay the Notch.

It was another half hour of rough going when the country imperceptibly started to close in on him, the land to each side reaching up precipitately into jagged peaks.

Still no fire, no sign of a camp. He cursed himself for a fool. Now he was in strange country, at night, not lost but just the same as lost, utterly helpless to change his predicament.

Blue caught his indecision and slowed. Shamrock reined him up, listening to the quiet of the night.

I'll shoot, he thought. *That might bring somethin'— maybe from the posse, though.*

But he flipped out his gun and shot twice into the air, listening to the echo beat its way up the canyon. No sound. He holstered his gun and lifted the reins.

Suddenly two shots, rifle shots, distinct and clear, answered him.

Blue whickered and started forward, when Shamrock pulled him up sharply and listened. A sound, a rumble, came above the night wind, and for a moment Shamrock could not interpret it. Then it hit him. The posse! It was the thunder of horses!

He spurred Blue in a blind, mad gallop in the direction from which the shots had come, letting Blue pick his own footing.

Hyatt was standing just outside the circle of the campfire, looking east, when Shamrock pulled Blue to a halt and slid out of the saddle. Nancy, Matt, and Maginnis were sitting at the campfire built in the lee of a flat-faced boulder.

"Saddle up!" Shamrock ordered him curtly. "There's a posse on my tail right now." He strode across to where the horses were staked out, talking on the way. "You, too, Lee. They'll hang you along with Mayo."

Matt and Hyatt understood the urgency in his tone, and ran to their gear.

"What's it about?" Matt said.

"Murder. Gillespie was tortured and killed and his bank robbed, and a key ring planted to hang the job on Mayo. The posse's right behind me."

Silently, all of them worked.

"What about Nancy?" Matt said.

"Stay here with her," Shamrock replied. "They may get ugly with you, but it won't come to gunplay. Mayo's the one they want, but they'll take Maginnis, too."

Shamrock was yanking the cinch tight on the pinto when Nancy's quiet voice spoke from beside him.

"This is the beginning, is it?"

"I reckon," Shamrock said tonelessly.

"From now on, it's the dodge for Mayo—and Lee?"

"Would you rather see them swinging from that big Navajo pine over there?" Shamrock asked quietly.

"You know I wouldn't. I—I just hate to see them run."

"We all hate to run," Shamrock said wryly. "Sometimes we have to."

"To fight another day?" Nancy asked.

"That's it," Shamrock said gently.

Hyatt was at her side now.

"Is it safe for her if she stays, Ireland?"

"There's bound to be some in that posse that won't stand for a woman bein' hurt," Shamrock replied. "But she'll have to stay and take her chance. They've got nothin' on Matt, either. He'll watch her."

"Let me go with you!" Nancy pleaded.

"No," Shamrock said flatly.

Then, before she could fathom the real concern in his voice, he said, "Come on, man. *Come on!*"

The lake was agreed upon as the meeting place for them if they succeeded in eluding the posse.

Maginnis, wide-eyed and excited, listened to everything in silence.

Shamrock turned to him. "Got a rifle?"

"Sure."

"Then we ride."

He led off west through the Notch, but as soon as they were well out of sight of the fire, he stopped.

"They'll likely figger we rode through the Notch here, won't they?" Shamrock asked Hyatt.

"Sure. Won't we?" Maginnis asked.

"Is there any other way over the mountains?"

"No trails," Hyatt said.

Shamrock silently weighed their chances. If they stayed

on the east slope of the Ritas, their chance of getting caught was doubled. But if they rode through the Notch to the west slope, they would be in waterless country. But most important of all, the plan slowly crystallizing in his mind demanded they remain close to the Notch.

He dismounted, went back to Maginnis's pony, and drew out the carbine.

"Ride straight up the south slope here," he told Hyatt. "We'll likely kill our horses doin' it, but I don't aim to be driven through the Notch. We'll stay on this slope."

"I was thinkin' the same thing," Hyatt said. "They'll have us out of the country for good if we don't."

Maginnis said, "Where you goin' with that rifle?"

"Back," Shamrock said grimly.

"Why?"

"I don't trust that Lobell. None of his outfit."

"Let's all go," Maginnis said.

"Just me," Shamrock said.

"Aw—"

"Just me," Shamrock repeated. "Three of us might give it away. And if they catch you, they'll string you, Lee. Lead the horses up the slope here, and if you hear the posse, keep quiet and let them ride through. Remember, one rock rollin' down that slope will give you away. Work your way up the slope as far as you can. I'll pick up your trail later. That's sense, isn't it, Hyatt?"

Hyatt, thus appealed to and knowing that he had the care of Maginnis, said it was, although a second before he had been determined to go with Shamrock.

But before either of them could protest or assent, Shamrock was gone in the dark. He worked his way back through the Notch and up the slope. When he saw the fire again, it was burning brightly, as if more fuel had been added.

With careful haste, he made for it. Nancy and Matt were sitting alone, both of them in position of tense alertness.

As Shamrock watched, Matt stood up and faced the east. Almost at once, the first horseman—Lobell—rode into the circle of firelight followed by the posse.

Shamrock cautiously made his way down as close as possible to the fire. Shielded from sight by a big boulder, with which the slope was thick-strewn, he got close enough so that he could hear. He had to hear, for he had the outlaw's fear of a posse and what otherwise sane men did when they were ganged together in a mob. A careless word from Matt, and one of them might work off all the anger and blood-lust of a night's fruitless riding.

Lobell had dismounted now, along with four or five other men.

"You say he was here?" the sheriff was inquiring flatly.

"There's his rope," Matt said, pointing to it beside Nancy's feet. "He was in sort of a hurry to go," he added dryly. His tone was calm, sturdily defiant.

"And I s'pose that young hellion of a Ireland come up and warned him?"

"I suppose," Matt said.

"Which way'd he go?" Gill, the rancher, blurted out.

"Up the slope," Matt said immediately.

"Huh-uh," Lobell said, some of the ugliness gone out of his voice.

"Did you think I'd tell you?" Matt drawled.

He stood there a little spraddle-legged in the center of the loose circle of men, his hands on his hips. Nancy, straight and scornful, stood beside and a little behind him.

"You stick up for him, and you know what he done?" Gill asked, his voice savage with anger.

"I know he never murdered a man in his life," Matt said staunchly. "That's good enough for me."

"And tortured him," Gill added.

"Not Hyatt. There's a heap of men I could name around here that would, but not him."

"Around here?" fat George blurted out. He took a step toward Matt, clearing himself of the crowd. "That sorta cuts it down, don't it?"

"That puts it up to about thirty men," Matt answered evenly.

Shamrock felt it coming and he raised his rifle to lay it over the rock. As he did so, his foot moved and stirred some loose rocks, which slid a few inches and stopped.

George looked up the slope.

"What's that?" he asked.

"That's him up there," Matt taunted. "Go up and get him."

George turned to him with a snarl, when Lobell's patient, fatherly voice cut in.

"Now, George. Easy." The sheriff reached in his pocket for the ever-present peppermint and put one in his mouth, then cuffed his Stetson back and looked at Nancy.

"I s'pose you're convinced your brother ain't a killer, too."

"I was with him all day," she retorted coldly. "Why shouldn't I be?"

The sheriff shook his head and turned to the posse. "Well, let's git goin'. If he rode up from town after murderin' Gillespie, then his horse is as tired as ours is. Unless," he added, turning to Matt, "he took yours."

"He did," Matt said.

"Did he pay you with Gillespie's bank money?"

"That's right," Matt taunted. "He left me some money to buy some pep'mint drops for the hull posse, too."

The sheriff cursed, and turned away.

"You goin' to leave 'em here?" Gill asked hotly. He cursed Matt. "I say, string him up!"

"You can say it, Gill, but don't try it," Matt advised coolly. "I ain't such a jughead I think I can fight thirty men. But there's two or three of 'em I can fight, and *will*."

"Leave him be, Gill!" a rider commanded. He was one of the more sober ranchers, of which there were a few in the posse. "He ain't goin' to tell us nothin' and neither is she. Every minute we spend here, Hyatt is ridin' from us. Come on."

It was this counsel that prevailed, and the men started for their horses. Lobell, however, surveyed Matt with deliberation.

"Matt, you and me have knowed each other a long time. I never liked the outfit you worked for, but I always tried to treat 'em like I would anybody else. Take my advice and high-tail it. You're free now because Hyatt has convicted hisself by runnin'. If he wasn't guilty, he'd of went back with us and stood trial like a man. But he is. Even you ain't blind to that. You got a chance to be somethin' on this range now and folks won't treat you like a suckegg dog. Turn over this here murderer to the law."

"To a bunch of men that was always scared to speak their mind to him face to face, huh?" Matt jeered. "I'd be likely to."

"You can't say you never had your chance, Matt," Lobell said patiently. "I need a deputy, a good head, an old head. Will you take it?"

"Not unless I was so drunk I took you for a stranger," Matt drawled.

"Come on, Andy," one of the posse said.

Lobell whirled and faced the speaker.

"Come where? Where? Can't you knotheads see he's gone?" he raged. "How can I get him if I don't know where he's went? In the dark! Two men runnin' from forty! Why, hell, both of them might be listenin' to me talk right now! Where'll we go?"

The proposition was sobering, and the men looked at each other questioningly.

"He's went through the Notch sure," one man said.

"How do you know?" Lobell cut in.

"He knows we'd pick him up sooner or later if he stuck on this slope. He's got money, and he's aimin' to high-tail it."

"It's two hours till daylight," another said. "Let's go through the Notch, rest our horses, and wait for daylight. Then we can fan out and trail for him."

The sheriff, suddenly amiable again, grunted and mounted his horse.

"It looks like that's what we got to do," he said grimly. "You boys are in for a long ride, and you'll be lucky if it ends short of the Territory line."

Without another look at Matt or Nancy, he spurred his horse off into the dark in the direction Shamrock and the others had gone only a few minutes before.

The posse, grim and silent, filed past the fire after him. Only one man spoke courteously to Matt and Nancy and raised his hat before darkness swallowed him. That was Scott, the man who had defied Soholt in the poker game at the Legal Tender.

As the last of them disappeared, Shamrock sat back and wiped the sweat from his forehead. If he had been dubious of Matt's ability to take care of Nancy he was reassured now. He thought of going down to them, but immediately decided against it. There was nothing to tell them, and Lobell would probably drop a man back to watch their campfire for the rest of the night.

For a minute Shamrock watched them. Nancy sat down, while Matt stirred the fire and put on more fuel, then went out to look at the horses.

Nancy sat alone, small in the light of the blazing fire. It gave dancing lights to her hair, like the moon does to water. She sat half turned to Shamrock, her legs crossed tailor-fashion, absently toying with a handful of gravel which she would pick up and sift through her fingers, then pick up again. As Shamrock watched her, some of the starch seemed to go out of her back and she hunched forward.

He knew what she was thinking. A home lost this day, tonight her brother on the outlaw trail again. Only now did Shamrock realize what she had probably bucked along with Matt in the absence of Mayo and her father. Tonight was the bitter end, the end she might have foreseen months back and which she had fought so passionately and futilely against. And now she was alone, except for Matt; homeless, no shelter, no land, no cattle, nothing—not even her brother.

Shamrock stood up, and was about to step down to her, when he checked himself.

"Hell, it's not for me," he muttered bitterly.

Maybe Nancy had heard that mumbled speech, for she called to Matt. He came over.

"I thought I heard someone speak up there," she said.

"Likely a couple of Lobell's men waitin' for Mayo," Matt said. "Let 'em wait."

Shamrock waited until the alarm had died, then sneaked back up the slope. In the dark, his face was more somber than he would have thought possible.

CHAPTER FOURTEEN

THE REST OF THE NIGHT was spent in work, hard, painstaking work that brought forth all the trail cunning of Shamrock and Hyatt. They were out to blot their trail. They circled far down to pick up the posse trail, then came back over it, trusting to its scuffed anonymity to hide their tracks. They left it twice on rock, came back to it, and only at the lake left it for good.

Here the posse had stopped to water their horses. Shamrock waded Blue into the shallow shore water, Hyatt and Maginnis behind him. They left the lake on a slope of granite that fingered out into the water, followed it to another rock outcrop, and wound in a perfect maze of confused direction until the rock petered out.

Then they headed for the peaks, Hyatt in the lead. The best man Lobell could put on their trail would spend two days on it even if he were to succeed and Hyatt knew that none of the ranchers would have the patience to persevere that long so close to home.

By daylight, they were high in the mountains, and a chill wind was blowing down from the peaks that the deep pines smothered, but did not hush.

It was here, just at sunrise, in the mouth of a small box canyon just below timber line and out of the wind that they camped. They could see the broad sweep of the country below just lifting its night shadows before the sun. Where they were, they got the sun first, and even as they watched the clean gold curtain of day fled down the mountainside, then into the foothills, then into the valley, throwing every ridge and wash into relief.

Shamrock knew in this wind and considering their position, it would not be foolish to build a small fire, and he instructed Maginnis to rustle hard, dry wood while he and Hyatt unsaddled and staked out the horses. They had two slickers and a single blanket between them for sleeping, and two pounds of jerky for food which had been left in Hyatt's saddlebag. The horses drank first from a clear, tiny mountain stream a hundred yards off and were staked out.

The three of them ate their jerky and stretched out in the light of the increasing sun, warmed by the meager food and fire and cigarettes.

Maginnis was drowsy, but he leaned back against a rock and looked at Shamrock.

"What do you aim to do now?"

"Sleep," Shamrock said, yawning. "I'll sleep for two hours, then Hyatt'll wake me. I'll call you in another two. Then we'll talk it over."

Shamrock winked at Hyatt as he got the blankets and slickers. Maginnis steadfastly refused the blanket and took the slickers. Shamrock lay down, Maginnis beside him.

Shamrock lay there for two minutes, then looked cautiously at Maginnis. The youngster was already deep in the sleep of exhaustion and Shamrock rose and gently put the blanket over him. Hyatt watched, too. Shamrock stood over Maginnis a moment, studying the face that lost some of its gravity in sleep and seemed younger. It was a good face, a little worn by work, but fine, lean, sensitive, the face of a thoroughbred. Shamrock looked over at Hyatt.

"Pretty young for coyote bait," he observed. "Well, Lobell hasn't got him yet."

"And won't," Hyatt said.

They moved over to the other side of the canyon, out of hearing, and sat down with their backs to warm rock. Each rolled a smoke lazily, comfortably.

"Did the kid tell you?" Shamrock asked, after lighting from Hyatt's match.

"All of it. That youngster's got plenty sand in his craw. Too much, I reckon. Maybe if he'd come to me we could have made medicine over this before."

"What do you make of it?"

"Tell me about Gillespie first."

Shamrock did so, mentioning again the key ring of the elder Hyatt that had been planted to convict Mayo of the robbery and murder.

"It would have been easy to get," Hyatt mused. "We left at noon, and since we couldn't take everything, we didn't take anything. A man watchin' the place could have got it and rode back to town."

"And Lobell was the only one besides his men who knew you were leaving and the place could be searched, so he got the key ring."

"You think Lobell killed Gillespie?"

"I don't think anything. You knew them both. What do you think?"

Hyatt was quiet a moment as he squirmed his back against the rock, scowling in thought. "I got a lot of ideas —but they don't add up." He paused. "If Lobell killed Gillespie, why did he do it?"

"To get the bank's money?" Shamrock suggested.

"Maybe," Hyatt answered. "But I always figured they were in together to get the Double Diamond. Lobell never raised a finger to keep our stuff from being rustled. Sometimes I've thought he and his men were doing the rustling themselves."

"What for, the cattle?"

"If it was only the cattle he was after, why would he want to kill me after they're gone?"

"Then he wanted the Double Diamond—all of it for himself," Shamrock said slowly. He looked at Hyatt. "Could he get it by killing Gillespie?"

Hyatt shrugged. "Gillespie owned the bank. He had no heirs. I suppose bank paper would go up for sale in the case of Gillespie's death, wouldn't it?"

Shamrock nodded. "So Lobell buys the Double Diamond with the money he stole from the bank. That's simple enough, isn't it?"

Hyatt looked at him and nodded. "Lobell just wanted the Double Diamond for himself."

Shamrock rolled and thoughtfully lighted a cigarette. "None of this explains the Maginnis business, though, and Lobell trying to get the kid." Shamrock scowled. "I keep wondering who old Maginnis's backer was."

Hyatt just looked at him, puzzled. Shamrock went on

then: "Let's make this real simple. You want money. Where do you go?"

"To a bank."

"Let's say Gillespie," Shamrock said slowly. "Maginnis goes to Gillespie, says he knows where there's gold. He proves it by showing him the samples, but he doesn't tell him the location for fear Gillespie would stake claims around all his, then tell him to go to hell for his backing. Finally they draw up the papers assuring old Maginnis of his share. As soon as the papers are signed, Maginnis tells him where the gold is. Then what happened?"

Hyatt scowled. "What did?"

"Your dad was killed. Maginnis was blamed for it and hung by a mob stirred up by Lobell's men. All right, say Gillespie and Lobell planned it so as to kill the only other man who knew the location of the gold." He spread his hands now. "But why kill your father?"

Hyatt just looked at him. "Maginnis's gold and the Double Diamond hook up together. Is that it? The gold is on Double Diamond land and that's why they want the ranch?"

"Couldn't be," Shamrock said flatly. "If Maginnis found the gold on the Double Diamond, what would he have done?"

Hyatt scowled. "Why, he would have come to Dad and offered him a fifty-fifty split, so they'd both make money."

"But he never did."

"No."

"Then the gold isn't on Double Diamond land," Shamrock said.

Hyatt shook his head wonderingly. "Then what's the connection between Maginnis's gold and the Double Diamond if the gold isn't on the ranch?"

"That's one for you to answer," Shamrock said quietly. "Try to think. There are other ranches and ranchers that

Lobell and Gillespie could have rustled to ruin and taken over. Yet they picked on your dad's spread. Why? What's it got that other ranches haven't?"

Hyatt was watching him and now he said promptly, "Water. More water than any other outfit. Even a lake."

He and Shamrock looked at each other, speculating. "Water," Shamrock murmured. "Gold." He shook his head wonderingly and then an expression of dawning enlightenment came into his face. "We're fools," he announced presently.

"How come?"

"There's plenty of connection between water and gold," Shamrock said. "I've been thinking all the time about a hard-rock gold mine. What's the matter with a placer mine?"

Hyatt nodded. "You need water to mine a placer claim."

"Sure," Shamrock said quickly. "Remember what young Lee told me this afternoon? He said when Maginnis rowed with your dad at the lake, he was filling water kegs and packing them on burros." He spread his hands. "That makes old Maginnis prospecting on the dry slope, on the west slope of the Ritas, doesn't it? Otherwise he could have hit the main stream and the feeder streams any place on the east slope."

Hyatt was looking at him. "What good would a lake high up on the east slope do Maginnis if his claims were on the west slope?"

Abruptly Shamrock said, "The lake's way below the Notch."

"Not much," Hyatt contradicted. "A hundred feet of solid rock, three or four miles long." Now Hyatt smiled and said softly, "I've got it."

Shamrock only shook his head. "No man's going to pack gravel up and over a mountain to wash it in a high lake."

"Ever hear of a siphon?" Hyatt asked softly. "Three miles of pipe over Double Diamond land, and the lake outlet would start flowing down the west slope."

They looked at each other almost in disbelief.

"Down to the land where old Maginnis found the gold," Shamrock finished. "Old Maginnis had to have that water. He didn't have the money to buy the Double Diamond to get the water to mine the gold. That's why he went to the bank, to Gillespie, to get the money."

Hyatt gestured briefly with one hand and shook his head. "That adds up all the way. Maginnis laid it in their laps. Once Lobell and Gillespie knew Maginnis's scheme, they set the wheels in motion. They killed my father, had Maginnis lynched for his murder, rustled the Double Diamond to ruin in the bank's hands, but when they finally got the Double Diamond, Lobell sees a way to keep it all, the ranch and the gold. He kills Gillespie, gets the money to buy the ranch, hangs the murder on me, and tries to kill young Lee. Once that's done, he's in the clear. He's the only man alive who knows where the gold lies and he'll get the water to mine it."

CHAPTER FIFTEEN

"Lordy!" an awed voice said.

Shamrock looked up to see Maginnis standing almost beside him. He and Hyatt had been so wrapped up in their talk that they had not heard him come up.

"You heard?" Shamrock said.

Maginnis, wide-eyed with wonder, nodded. "And Lobell done all that? Figgered that all out?"

"He did," Hyatt said grimly, looking up at Maginnis.

"At least we know why we're goin' to kill him, Lee."

"But not yet," Shamrock put in.

"Why not?" Maginnis said.

"You goin' to wait for him on a trail, kid?" Shamrock asked. "You goin' to shoot him, then dump him in a dry gulch?"

Maginnis flushed. "No. But he deserves it—worse than that."

"Let him hang himself," Shamrock said quietly. "He will. He'll let this posse run itself out, then things will quiet down. After that, the first thing he'll do is to get his stakes out on that gold. He'll do it quiet—and right away."

"But it ain't his!" Maginnis cried. "We goin' to let him do it?"

"Do you know where it is?" Shamrock countered.

"No."

"Then let him lead us to it. He's the only one that knows. If he don't take us there, no one ever will."

"But it's got to be down the slope," Lee said.

"And that's a lot of land," Shamrock reminded him.

"We've got it narrowed down, anyway," Hyatt said. "Once that water gets over the Notch, there's only one place it can run—unless he aims to pipe it for miles and miles. There's a gut runnin' most of the way down that slope. Everything drains into it. It's deep as Gehenna, too. The claims would have to lie below that."

"But that still leaves considerable ground."

"Considerable," Hyatt said, smiling.

Shamrock built a cigarette, lighted it, looking off at the flats below. For the first time since he had ridden into the country, he knew the right value of things, and of the people. It was a war in the open now, the three of them here against anyone Lobell chose to send against them. It was a feeling he had long been used to—this life. Yet it was different, too, for he had young Maginnis to think of.

Shamrock was determined to leave the kid free, with no Lobell to harry him, and in possession of what was rightly his. And down below, too, was Nancy. Shamrock had the uneasy feeling that sooner or later she would be drawn into this, drawn into it with such catastrophic violence that they would be defeated in the end. Lobell wouldn't kill her, Shamrock knew, for the sheriff was not such a fool as to believe he could get away with that. The entire country would spend a lifetime hunting him down. But there were other things, such as using her as a decoy for Mayo, or kidnaping her, that had to be considered. But that was preferable to having her with them, facing ambush and sudden death at every turn of the trail. Only Matt, tough and defiant, was there to protect her.

And then he suddenly wondered why he should think of her at all. She had called him a killer, had blamed him for dragging Mayo back to the outlaw life, had even accused him of being in Lobell's pay. He felt his face grow hard again as he thought of her. She wasn't his kind anyway, and the only reason he regarded her was because of Mayo. He threw his cigarette away and yanked himself down to realities.

"There's only one way he's liable to get into it, isn't there?"

"The Notch?"

Shamrock nodded. "That's why I didn't aim to have them chase us over onto the west slope. We'll camp at the Notch. Maybe it won't be Lobell that'll come, but it'll be one of his men. And they'll show us the spot."

"When?" Maginnis asked eagerly.

"Tomorrow. That's why I wanted you to get some sleep, kid. Lobell will spend most of the day lettin' that posse ride itself out. By night, if we have any luck, they'll have lost us and headed for home. Tomorrow, things'll be quiet, and Lobell will start his prowlin'. It's goin' to take some stayin' awake, Lee."

"Let's go," Maginnis said.

Shamrock rose and stretched, then tousled Lee's hair with rough affection.

"Back to the blankets—the lot of us. We go at midafternoon and get there by midnight."

It was a starvation camp that night at the west end of the Notch, both for horses and men. Where the Notch funneled out onto the west slope, the land was broken, a gaunt, upthrown country of savage rock and canyon, a waterless and harsh labyrinth of badlands that sloped down to the desert below.

A half mile from the Notch, they found a camping place where a few stunted piñon had laid a thin carpet of needles on the rock. There was no fire built, no food eaten, and their horses, after the exhausting travel of the afternoon on the rocky terrain at timber line, needed grass. But they, too, went hungry.

Maginnis, weary but stubbornly cheerful, was tolled off to stay at camp, while Shamrock took a rifle and settled himself at the Notch to wait and listen, listen and wait through the long hours before dawn. Hyatt rode the five miles through the pass and down to the lake to see if Matt and Nancy were there and had any news of the posse.

At dawn, Maginnis came to spell Shamrock, who willingly gave over.

Back at camp, Hyatt sat on a rock with a slicker before him loaded with jerky, a tin of coffee—useless, because they dared not build a fire—and some cold biscuits and a canteen of water.

"Matt cached this stuff where I'd be sure to find it at a place he used to take me fishin' when I was a kid," Hyatt explained.

"They gone?"

Hyatt nodded. "Matt figgered it might look too suspicious, I reckon. Lobell likely had a man watchin' them. I looked there in the cache on the hunch he might've left a note, but he didn't."

"Find any more of the posse's tracks?"

"They come back," Hyatt said. "I didn't go down to see if they picked up our trail, but they rode back through the pass."

Shamrock took Maginnis's portion of grub to him, with the final instructions that if anyone came through the Notch, he was to let him go and come back and wake the camp.

Dog-tired, Hyatt and Shamrock ate, then rolled away under the piñons and with a slicker for cover, dropped immediately into the sleep of the dead.

When Maginnis woke him around noon, Shamrock could see the youngster was excited.

"They've come!"

"Who?"

"Freed and another man. They just rode through."

Hyatt was awakened and they saddled up, but in no particular hurry. It was decided that Shamrock should go first, so that if Freed and the other man happened to be watching their back trail and Shamrock walked into them, Maginnis and Hyatt would be able to rescue him.

Shamrock looked at Maginnis with troubled eyes as he swung up on Blue. "You're goin' against gunmen, kid. You know that?"

Maginnis nodded grimly and his hand fell to the butt of his Colt. "It won't be the first time I've handled a Colt," he said.

Shamrock caught Hyatt's look of understanding, and as he rode away he knew Hyatt could and would do the gunfighting for both.

Shamrock played cautious. Heading down the deep canyon that twisted and writhed down the slope between high canyon walls, he watched the arroyo bottom. The tracks of the posse were here, though not many of them, and although he could get an impression of the tracks of the riders ahead, they were not clear.

He loafed, watching the canyon walls keenly and rounding the tortuous bends of the stream bed with caution. At last, far down, in midafternoon, he saw where the posse had collected and turned back. The country sloped out a bit here, and the canyon walls had diminished, so that he could see some of the surrounding country. Still it was rough, and desert.

He followed the tracks on until he saw where the two riders had crossed some hard-packed sand wind-drift. Here he dismounted and studied the tracks. He was taking no chances of losing them if they crossed with some of the posse outriders farther down.

Then he doubled the caution with which he rode. It didn't matter how far the two riders were ahead of him. If he could follow them, that was all he wanted.

Suddenly, abruptly, the canyon funneled out into rolling country that was dry and shimmering in the afternoon sun. Only an odd patch of greasewood and an occasional yucca relieved the monotony of the rock and sand and gravel. *Sahuaro* and *ocotillo* were almost plentiful, and far above in the cloudless sky a buzzard wheeled in lazy inspection, then passed on to better grounds.

Off to the left, there was a low hogback, bare and flinty, and the tracks turned almost at right angles and headed for it. Shamrock approached it doubtfully. Over the hump, Freed and his companion might be waiting, or resting. But to skirt it meant having to leave the tracks and pick them up again on flinty ground. He decided to chance it. A dozen yards from the top, he reined Blue up and looked back. Hyatt and Maginnis were not in sight. He left Blue's reins trailing and worked his way to the top in the direction of a clump of sagebrush. Before he reached it, he removed his Stetson, bellied down, and crawled up behind the sage.

There, just down the slope in a small *rincon* formed by wind erosion where a lower ridge joined the hogback at right angles, were Freed and his companion—dismounted. They were squatting together, a map laid on the ground before them. Harmer was the other man.

Shamrock smiled a little, but made no move. Freed was gesturing and arguing, when abruptly he pointed in Shamrock's direction. Harmer seemed to agree, and they rose. Harmer kept the map, while Freed turned, faced Shamrock, and started walking, as if counting his steps.

He was coming up the slope, headed so as to miss Shamrock by only ten feet. Shamrock drew his gun and hunkered lower behind the sagebrush.

Freed slogged up the hill head down, reached the hump, and crossed it. Still he had not looked up, had not seen Shamrock a dozen feet away, nor Blue.

Shamrock, still lying down, moved his foot over some pebbles. The noise jerked Freed out of it with a start, and he looked over into the barrel of Shamrock's gun.

"Don't yell," Shamrock said softly. "Don't move, either."

Freed nodded, licking his lips.

"Call him," Shamrock ordered.

Freed hesitated a moment, and Shamrock nosed up his gun.

"Harmer," Freed called. "Come here."

Shamrock waited, listening for Harmer's footsteps, not taking his eyes from Freed.

Harmer was laboring up the slope now. Shamrock saw the top of his Stetson first, then his face, then his shoulders, and then Harmer looked up and stopped.

"That blue—"

Shamrock stood up from behind the sagebrush, his gun

leveled at Harmer.

Harmer caught the movement out of the corner of his eye and his hand instinctively started down.

"Don't!"

Harmer was no fool. He thrust his hands in the air and turned to face Shamrock.

Stepping out of the sagebrush, and keeping Harmer between himself and Freed, he walked over and flipped their guns out on the ground and kicked them away.

"I thought you two slept in the daytime," he jeered quietly.

Freed opened his mouth to speak, then gulped his words back.

"Go ahead," Shamrock invited him.

"We're lookin' for Hyatt," Freed said.

"With a map? Maybe you'd like a compass and a couple of pack horses, too?"

Freed glanced at Harmer, then shrugged and settled into sullen silence.

"Step over here," Shamrock ordered Freed. Then he searched him, and found a knife which he threw down with the guns. A search of Harmer revealed nothing.

"Now let's go down and make medicine," Shamrock said.

"Where?"

"To the map. Isn't that it down there all spread out with rocks weightin' it down—or is that an oilcloth you aimed to eat on?"

Reluctantly, Freed and Harmer went back down the hill. Shamrock first backed them against the wall of the *rincon* away from both the map and their horses.

"Now just turn around and look at the rock," he said grimly. "I'll be busy for a minute."

He walked over to the map, his glance on them both, then squatted and let his gaze fall to the map.

It was a blank piece of paper.

"Just get busy but don't move!" a voice commanded him from behind. Lobell's!

For a second he paused, cursing himself for falling into this simple trap, wondering if he could fight it out.

"It's a rifle," Lobell said. "It's square on your backbone. I wouldn't try it if I was you."

Freed and Harmer had turned around now and were grinning as they watched him.

"Make a move," Harmer dared him.

It was hopeless. Before he could move, Lobell would send a slug into his back. His face was hard and still as he flipped his gun to the ground.

Freed and Harmer pounced on it while Shamrock rose and turned. Lobell had been forted up just over the low ridge, and, as he said, he had a rifle trained on Shamrock.

He moved lazily down to Shamrock now, levering all the shells from his gun and tossing it aside. His walk was slow, stately, marred only by his gesture of reaching in his pocket for a peppermint drop and slipping it into his mouth.

"That was good, boys," he said to Freed and Harmer, like a father meting out sober praise to his sons. "Mighty good. I almost believed it myself."

And now he regarded Shamrock with quiet curiosity. "You've got a good head," he said slowly. "Trouble with you is, you never give other people credit for havin' the sense you got."

"They don't have," Shamrock said flatly.

The sheriff smiled tolerantly. "Reckon you got the head to get out of this?"

"I'll get out," Shamrock said.

Deliberately, Lobell drew his gun and held it loosely in his hand. "Not unless you can dodge this slug."

"You won't shoot," Shamrock said. "Someone might

hear it."

"That's right, too," Lobell said, holstering his gun. "You see, I got the sense to listen to other people. If you was to live twenty years longer, you might."

"I will," Shamrock said arrogantly.

The sheriff shook his head. "No, you won't. I can't promise many things, but I reckon I can promise you that. You won't live more'n an hour longer."

Shamrock's lip lifted in a sneer.

"That's right," Lobell said. "Get salty. I like 'em that way."

Shamrock squatted on his heels against the rock and rolled a smoke.

"Just what did you think you'd find here on this paper?" the sheriff asked casually. "What was you lookin' for?"

"A recipe for fruit cake," Shamrock said.

Lobell walked over slowly to him, and faced him. "Sonny, it's about time you got the edge took off you. Answer my questions."

Shamrock made an unprintable sound and lighted his cigarette.

"Where's Maginnis and Hyatt?"

"You're huntin' 'em," Shamrock said.

"That roan come in," the sheriff said amiably. "I found the two bodies. Maginnis was likely with Hyatt when we missed them up in the Notch. Where are they?"

Shamrock said nothing, just looked insolently at the sheriff.

"Didn't I tell you once I didn't like that face?" Lobell asked softly.

"You wouldn't be the first one."

"I'll be the first one that ever tried to change it," Lobell said. And without warning, he kicked Shamrock in the face. It caught Shamrock on the cheek and slammed his head back against the rock, and a thousand stars rocketed in front of the blackness in his eyes. That was all he knew.

When Shamrock was wakened, it was by some one throwing water in his face.

Lobell was standing over him with a canteen, and, after regarding him a moment with benevolent impersonality, said, "That's that drink of mine you turned down the day I met you. Want another?"

Shamrock shook his head. His eyes were still jeering, and the sheriff noticed it.

"It don't matter, son," he said pleasantly. "They'll be along and we'll gather them in."

Then he turned to Freed. "Go git his blue and bring him over here. Leave him ground-haltered by this paper."

He drew his gun, then said to Shamrock, "Harmer and me'll take you with us."

Shamrock was prodded up the ridge, then down its far slope. There, halfway down it, was a short tunnel that went ten feet into the ridge. Shamrock guessed immediately it was an old test pit of the elder Maginnis. Somewhere around here might be the gold-bearing land.

"Wonderin' what it is?" Lobell asked.

"I know."

"I thought you did."

Shamrock was prodded back into the tunnel and sat down with his back against the end of it. Harmer and the sheriff sat in silence until Freed came up, then Lobell gave his instructions.

"Sometimes I git pretty rough," he began, "but what I *have* been ain't even a half of what I *will* be if you let him get six feet from the mouth of this tunnel. If he moves, cut down on him. Give him everything you got. Make sure. I'd like to have him whole for them others to see, but I ain't particular. You got it, Freed?"

Freed nodded.

"Have you, George?"

Harmer nodded too.

"Good. Remember it, because I mean it."

And he left without another word. Freed and Harmer were sufficiently impressed by his warning. They both drew guns and sat almost side by side facing Shamrock. He was looking out at daylight, while they were looking at darkness, so that they could see his face while he could not see theirs. He knew what they were thinking—of Soholt, of Pace, of the bluff at the Double Diamond, of the rescue of Maginnis, of the death of the two guards, of the jail-key steal, and of Hyatt's escape. He knew they hated him for making fools of them, and that they would rather shoot him than not—much rather. He thought, too, that this was the end of his rope. Lobell had planned it neatly. He had given Shamrock the credit for having brains enough to fit all the pieces together and to understand why the Double Diamond was so valuable. The sheriff had figured, and rightly, that with Maginnis's story and Hyatt's, it would take only a little astuteness and patience to work out the whole scheme. And he knew that Shamrock, essentially a man of action, would not sit by and see it done. So he had sent Freed and Harmer through the Notch as decoys, making it look as if he were out to get the land immediately while Hyatt and Shamrock were shaking the posse. He knew that Shamrock could shake the posse, and after doing it would watch the Notch for him.

So he had forted up down here away from everyone, close to logical location of the gold, and had waited for Shamrock to walk into his trap. Hyatt and Maginnis would follow as a matter of course. It was cunning. Lobell had thought things out just a little farther, a little more carefully, and the game was his. When Hyatt and Maginnis came in and were caught, then Lobell would have everyone he wanted.

He would line them up and shoot them with never a

quiver of nerve or conscience.

Harmer brought him back to more immediate danger by saying to Freed, "Let's let him have it. Andy don't care."

Freed thought a moment. "Better not. He'd like to have him with the others."

"We'll say he tried to escape."

Freed chuckled. "Hell. Why not wait for the others? I'd like to see them all together."

"*Bueno,*" Harmer said, and laughed, too. "How does it sound, hardcase?"

"Bad," Shamrock said.

"I told you."

"Yeah. But I'm not dead yet."

Harmer, cursing, raised a gun, but Freed beat it down quickly.

"Easy, Harmer. He'll get it."

So they sat in silence. Shamrock pictured Hyatt and Maginnis following his tracks, stopping just over the ridge where he dismounted from Blue. Hyatt would be careful, and he would cast about for more sign, finally coming on Freed's and Harmer's tracks where Shamrock disarmed them. They would be hard to read any meaning into, but even if Hyatt succeeded he would approach the top of the ridge silently, probably in the same clump of sagebrush, and see Blue standing there alone. The natural thing to think would be that Shamrock had dismounted either to scout ahead, or, if he had prisoners, gone off to look for claim corners. Then Hyatt and Maginnis would walk down to Blue—and into the sheriff's trap. It was dead end, all right.

He had a cigarette half rolled when he heard a whistle.

Freed looked at Harmer. "He's got 'em." He turned to Shamrock. "Come out of here."

Harmer and Freed backed out, and Shamrock came after them. They were watching him, daring him to make a break, but Shamrock saw how hopeless it was. They didn't even get close enough to allow him a chance of grabbing a gun. He turned and walked up the slope, finishing the building of his cigarette.

Maginnis and Hyatt were disarmed, backed against the rock. Shamrock was prodded over to them, where he lit his cigarette and squatted. Maginnis had stark fear in his eyes, so there was no sense of Shamrock's pretending it wasn't serious. Hyatt's face was hard, drained of color, and his eyes were as wicked as a cornered wildcat's. He, too, rolled a smoke and squatted.

"Well, here we are, Lobell," Hyatt said calmly. "It looks like a showdown."

"Don't do it," Lobell said. He stood about ten feet from them, his carbine slacked off his shoulder. Harmer and Freed had six-guns out.

"How does it look?" the sheriff purred.

"I made a mistake," Hyatt said. "I should have listened to what Nancy had to say about you, then rode in town for a shoot-out."

"I reckon," the sheriff said pleasantly, and laughed a little. He fumbled in the brown paper sack that peeked from his vest pocket and pulled out a peppermint which he slipped into his mouth.

"Did you ever take a man's word for anything?" Hyatt asked him quietly.

"Once. Gillespie's."

"Would you again?"

"Depends."

"Will you take Ireland's word that if you give him and Maginnis horses, he'll ride to Montana with the kid and stay there and never come back?"

"Not me," Shamrock said quickly. "I'd come back. Let the kid go."

But Hyatt looked steadily at Lobell. "Would you? Why

154

toll them into my hard luck? I'm the man you want."

"I'd sure like to," Lobell said amiably. "Yes, sir, I'd sure like to. But I can't. You can see for yourself. It wouldn't be good business." He paused and studied them, his face bland and benevolent and kindly. "I sort of hate to hurt Ireland. He plays the kind of hand I like. But you heard him yourself. He'd come back. As for Maginnis, I just can't afford to."

And then his face washed out; all the false dignity and calmness, the air of the irreproachable patriarch had fled, leaving his face savage and cruel and predatory.

He hefted his gun easily. "You asked for it—the bunch of you. I'll start with you, Ireland. I hate your guts worse than the other two put together."

Shamrock, white-faced, said nothing, but his eyes still jeered, still mocked. He threw his cigarette away. "Let's have it."

Still Lobell did not move. He stood still for five long seconds, relishing it.

"Get it over with!" Maginnis cried furiously, his hands fisted until they were white.

But Lobell was watching Hyatt, and he saw an expression of slow amazement come over Hyatt's face as he looked over Lobell's shoulder to the hogback.

Lobell laughed. "I ain't goin' to turn around and have you dive for a gun, Hyatt. Harmer, you and Freed don't move."

Then Hyatt called, "Hello, Sis!"

And strangely, there was an answer.

"Hello."

Lobell, quick as thought, whirled, but Freed and Harmer stood still, covering them.

There, on the hogback, was Nancy on her horse, and beside her was Scott, Shamrock's poker companion of the first night in town. He was silent, curious.

"Why, howdy," the sheriff said carefully, cautiously. Shamrock hung his head, weak from fear and excitement. He stared at the ground, trying to compose his face, trying to believe.

He heard Maginnis's long intake of breath, half sob, half cry of joy.

CHAPTER SIXTEEN

It took Lobell only a moment to find himself.

"Why, hello, Scott," he called. "Come down."

Nancy and Scott rode down the slope and dismounted. Still, Freed and Harmer had not moved. Scott looked them over curiously, his manner puzzled.

"I thought you was with the posse," Lobell said to him.

"I was," Scott replied. His frank, honest gaze settled on the sheriff, and he explained. "Miss Hyatt stopped me last night when the posse rode past the lake. She missed you, and she asked me where you were. I told her the tracks seemed to split and that you'd taken one while we took the rest. She thought there'd be gunplay if you and her brother met, so I told her we'd find you and see."

"Oh," Lobell said, very quietly. "Well, that's fine. Uh— how'd you find me?"

"Tracked you," Scott answered slowly. "You didn't take the canyon down, did you?"

"No. I left it."

"I know. It was hard trackin'. Took most of the day." He turned from the sheriff to survey the prisoners again.

"Got 'em, huh?" he said grimly, no sympathy in his voice.

"No trouble at all," the sheriff replied. His gaze for the

first time shuttled to Nancy, and he lifted his hat courteously. Nancy ignored him, and started for Mayo when
the sheriff held out an arm to bar her.

"Wait a minute, miss." She stopped and faced him. "I'm
not havin' you talk to them, or them to you. Understand?"

"Why?"

"Why? How do I know what you'll tell 'em, or what
you'll plan? Where's Matt? He might be aimin' to stage a
rescue and you carry the word to them."

It was a shrewd stroke, Shamrock saw, for even Nancy
had not understood how close she had come to seeing them
all dead under Lobell's guns. And the sheriff didn't aim
to have her find out from conversation with her brother.

"Where's Matt?" Nancy repeated scornfully. "I suppose
you don't know?"

"Maybe I should, but I don't," Lobell admitted.

"He's dead!" Nancy blazed.

All of them were silent for a moment, then Scott said,
"Dead? But he was alive when the posse talked with you
last night."

"We moved down to the lake," Nancy explained, looking at Mayo, for he was the only one she cared to explain
it to. "Someone shot him in the back when he was staking
the horses out."

"But why didn't you tell me?" Scott asked gently. "When
you came over to the posse when we were watering the
horses, you never mentioned it."

"And why should I?" Nancy blazed. "It was someone
in the posse that did it! Lobell's men! You're all Lobell's
men!"

Scott kept silent, but he flushed under the smart of her
words. Nancy noticed it and made an impulsive gesture.

"I'm sorry, Mr. Scott. That wasn't kind of me. You've
helped me today"—she looked steadily at Lobell—"more
than you'll ever know."

And she turned and started for Mayo, but again the sheriff barred her way.

"I'm sorry about that—about Matt, but it don't change things. I'll not have you talkin' with prisoners. Either you keep still or off you ride, young lady. Take your choice. Come to think of it, Scott, I think you better take her home. This ain't pleasant for her."

"Home," Nancy said dryly, and the sheriff blushed at his slip.

"You stick," Shamrock put in quietly.

Lobell whirled to face him. "That goes both ways, Ireland. Do I have to gunwhip you to make you believe it?"

"You stick," Shamrock repeated to Nancy.

The sheriff took a swift step toward him, but Shamrock laughed at him. He knew how Lobell must act before an audience, and he knew he wouldn't dare do anything as long as Scott, an honest rancher, and Nancy, Mayo's sister, were along. The sheriff relaxed, but his mild voice carried the threat he meant it to.

"The next time you open your mouth, sonny, I'll stick a gag in it."

Shamrock nodded, for he could see Lobell meant it.

"What is that boy doing here?" Scott said. He had noticed Maginnis, who was sitting against the rock again, his face pale, but his eyes wide and alert and curious.

"He's a killer," Lobell explained. "Runnin' with his kind. He's wanted in Sahuaro County for murder. He's wanted here, too, for killin' two of my men—shootin' them in the back—and escapin'." He plucked at his underlip thoughtfully. "They're all killers," he continued reflectively. "Three young men, could have made somethin' of their lives in this country if they hadn't went bad. Take Ireland there. I got a poster yesterday announcin' there's five thousand on his head. He killed a deputy U.S. marshal up in Montana Territory. Maginn—McKinley there, he stuck up a bank and killed a cashier. And Hyatt." He shrugged. "You know why we're after him. Bad men—to a man."

Scott nodded soberly. Suddenly Nancy laughed. It was mostly hysteria, hysteria at what she had gone through and what she knew about Lobell, who had made this pious reflection on the ways of mankind. She went into gales and gusts of laughter until she cried. Lobell flushed and turned to Scott.

"You better take her away. She's upset."

"Oh, please, do," Nancy gasped. "So you can kill them all—these bad, bad men—and say they all jumped on you and tried to murder you!"

Lobell gave up, for he could sense that Nancy's ridicule was strengthening Scott's determination to ride with them. Freed and Harmer, stolid and blindly obedient to Lobell's instructions, had never taken their gaze from the three by the rock.

Curtly now, Lobell ordered Freed to round up all the horses. He held a gun on them now, his eyes smoldering, but he had not forgotten himself so far as to forget his peppermint, and he slipped one in his mouth and sucked on it placidly, his gaze on Shamrock.

It wasn't over, Shamrock knew. Lobell had an ace up his sleeve, and he would play it the way he played it before with old Maginnis. Jail—then lynching. This time it wouldn't be hard, for feeling was high against them. They had, perhaps, a day's grace, and then nothing but a miracle could save them. He looked at Hyatt, and saw that he had come to the same conclusion. Maginnis, too, had seen it immediately without the sheriff's having to announce that he was taking them to jail, and he looked at Shamrock.

For no reason in the world except that lightheartedness of a man who has just been reprieved from death, Shamrock smiled. Maginnis grinned back.

Nancy had stopped her laughing now, and stood watching the proceedings. Scott turned in to help the sheriff. Shamrock was taken first, ordered to mount, then his feet were tied under Blue's belly. Hyatt and Maginnis followed.

Then the procession started, Shamrock in the lead. A rope lay loosely around his shoulders, the end of it in the sheriff's hands. Maginnis and Hyatt were put in between the deputies, while Scott and Nancy brought up the rear.

They rode for the most part in silence until far after dark when they reached the lake. As they were drinking their horses, Hyatt asked Lobell, "Give us time off to bury Matt. He deserves that."

"Why, sure," Lobell said immediately, sadly. "He was a good man—a real good man. He died for people that wasn't worth it."

They found Matt just away from the shore of the lake, face down in the grass, the end of a picket rope still in his hand. He was carried to the shore of the lake, and stones piled on him. A rough pine-log headstone marked the rougher grave.

Then they camped. Freed and Harmer spelled Scott and the sheriff at guard while Nancy and the prisoners slept.

Shamrock slept little during the night. He lay there looking up at the stars, not wondering about his past life, for that was water under the bridge, but about the present. He turned over a dozen different plans of escape in his mind, and discarded them. Right now his feet were hobbled, his hands tied securely, and ten feet away beside the fire Lobell sat wide awake. Any break would be suicide. And the other alternative was just as inexorable. Once in jail, they would be lynched. Shamrock was not a man who, deprived of his gun, was a craven, but he longed for a gun now and the last red chance to blast his way free or die in the attempt.

But that won't work, either, he mused. *There's Maginnis*

and Mayo. He thought of Nancy, too, but he didn't say her name even in his mind. It would be worst for her, because she would have to go through the nightmare of watching it run its inevitable course, powerless to stop it. And she was powerless, for although Lobell had been careful to disguise it, she was being watched as closely as her brother. Lobell hadn't forgotten the time she roped and dragged him.

No, all of them were without friends—except for this Scott, who had been decent to Nancy from some innate courtesy. But he, too, believed them killers, and would not hesitate to shoot if they tried to escape. He would disapprove of a lynching, and would fight to bring them to justice, but one man—or a half-dozen men—in the face of a mob could do little.

Shamrock flogged his mind until it was weary, but every scheme tallied up the same—except one. He thought about that one for two hours, and finally decided that, insane as it seemed, utterly impossible as a fairy tale, it was their only chance. So far, he had matched Lobell lie for lie, deception for deception, cunning for cunning, until he had come to wonder if he could ever think or talk straightforwardly again. But this, this last hope, was a more gigantic deception, a more cunning lie than he had ever believed could be told, much less swung.

But I'll try it, he mused, with the wry distaste of a man who has never bothered to lie because he was not afraid of the truth.

So help me, I'll try.

And he turned over to sleep. As he was drowsing off, it suddenly occurred to him that the whole thing depended on Lobell's appointing one of two men for guard at the jail. It depended solely on luck, then. That was all right. Shamrock went immediately to sleep, for he was lucky, and he knew it.

CHAPTER SEVENTEEN

THE RIDE TO TOWN was slow and interminable, for Lobell was playing it cautious. They reached Malpais Springs at suppertime, and had not got past the town limits before their strange cavalcade started to attract a crowd. Youngsters followed it, while their elders hastened to spread the word.

At the sheriff's office, the prisoners were untied and taken singly into the jail and held in the corridor while Harmer rode down to the blacksmith's to see if the new keys were ready. Lobell had ordered wax impressions taken and a whole new set of keys filed. Shamrock cursed when he remembered that the original set was still wrapped in the bandanna clutched by the hand of Maginnis's guard. But keys alone would not get them out of this jail, he knew.

Harmer returned with the finished keys and Shamrock, Hyatt, and Maginnis were each put in a separate cell on the same side of the building, Shamrock in the middle.

As the door clanged shut, he could hear the excitement of the town, and he reflected bitterly that this time Lobell wouldn't have to start the lynching talk himself. Nancy stood with Scott in the corridor as the last door clanged shut.

"May I talk to Mayo now?" she asked Lobell coldly.

"I reckon," Lobell answered generously. "I'll go out and rustle some grub for them. Scott, you stay here with Harmer and Freed. As soon as I can, I'm goin' to deputize some good heads here in case anyone thinks they can start trouble."

"Good idea," Scott said.

"Then I'm goin' to hold that inquest over Gillespie," Lobell continued, and he looked at Hyatt. "There ain't any doubt, but it should be got on record." He turned and called, "Freed!"

Shamrock listened now, his heart beating fast as Freed came in.

"Git a chair, a shotgun, a rifle, a lantern, and camp in this corridor till I tell you to move." And he added, "You better do a better job of it than Pace done."

Shamrock settled back on his cot content. Scott went out, leaving Nancy standing alone in the corridor. She walked slowly to the bars of Hyatt's cell.

"What's going to happen, Mayo? What I think will?"

"The same thing that happened to Lee's dad," Hyatt said, looking through Shamrock's cell to Maginnis's. The youngster was standing with his hands on the partition bars, listening. His wrists and big hands were stuck far out of his shirt sleeves, his angular, unfleshed body was bent with fatigue, and his face was pinched and pale. His eyes were calm and untroubled, but there was something else in them that made Shamrock look away.

"Then—I'm going to kill Lobell," Nancy said calmly.

"That won't do it, sis." Hyatt shook his head in affectionate reproof. "It would get you jailed and make the town surer they want to hang us."

"But what *can* I do?" Nancy cried. "I can't stand by and see it done! Isn't there anyone that will believe me? They've got to! I've got to tell them!"

"Scott," Shamrock said.

"But he believes Hyatt killed Gillespie. I've talked to him. He thinks I'm wrong about Lobell, even."

"Keep talking to Scott," Shamrock said quietly. "Stick with him. Get out and talk. Hunt up the big men in this county, in this town. Tell them. Talk until you're sick, and talk some more."

Nancy looked at him curiously, and came over to his cell. "Look up here," she said.

He looked up at her and saw a strange gentleness behind the worry in her face.

"Why have you done this?" she asked. "For us—Lee and us?"

"I couldn't do anything else," Shamrock said.

"You could have ridden off a dozen times," Nancy contradicted. "You could have ridden off last night, yet you stuck with us. Why?"

"Call it for fun," Shamrock said wryly.

"It's no fun to know you're going to die."

"Well, that question always comes up sometime."

Nancy looked at him searchingly. "You don't believe in being serious even about serious things, do you?"

"No," Shamrock agreed.

"I do," Nancy said gravely. "I'm serious when I say I wish I could repay you for what you've done for us."

"Maybe it's payment enough just knowing you," he went on. "All the girls I've ever known were the wrong kind. The right kind I just read about in newspapers. I never believed they were real." He hesitated. "Now I know they are, and that's payment enough."

Nancy turned away, too filled with emotion to listen longer.

Now Lobell strode through the door, Harmer and a Chinese behind him carrying loaded trays of food.

Nancy turned back to Shamrock, put her hand through the bars, and Shamrock took it gently, awkwardly.

"Thank you," she said simply, and turned to go out. "I'll be back," she called over her shoulder.

The food was put in their cells. Freed came in with his chair, lantern, and two guns. He sat down inside the corridor door where Pace had sat on a similar occasion. He had a toothpick in his mouth and was sucking on it complacently, as the sheriff went out.

Shamrock sat quietly on his cot, the image of Nancy as she left the jail in his mind. He did not eat, but sat there staring at the blanket until Maginnis said, "Got the makin's?"

Shamrock pulled himself together and grinned at Maginnis, then handed him his Durham sack. He ate then, wolfing his meal.

Finished, Shamrock rolled a smoke and stretched out on his cot, watching Freed.

"I got a piece of pie left," he drawled lazily. "Anybody want it?"

Maginnis said he didn't, and so did Hyatt.

"Do you, Freed?"

"Keep it," Freed said.

Shamrock chuckled. "Get tough," he said easily. "It's the last piece of pie we'll get." He paused a second, then added distinctly, "All of us."

"Gettin' spooked?" Freed jeered.

"Sure. Aren't you?"

Freed looked at him a second before he answered. "Me?" he laughed softly. "I don't aim to fight very hard."

Shamrock looked at the ceiling and did not speak for a while, then said, "Huh-uh. That won't help you, Freed."

Hyatt, lying on his cot like Shamrock, was the first to understand that there was something behind Shamrock's lazy conversation. Shamrock could tell by his utter stillness that he was listening, and listening hard.

Shamrock didn't say anything for a full minute, pretending he was listening to the growing, angry mutter outside, but he was watching Freed. Over the jailer's face came a mild look of inquiry, a frown almost, and he picked his teeth idly as he studied Shamrock.

"It won't help me?" he slowly repeated Shamrock's statement. "I don't savvy it."

"You wasn't meant to," Shamrock said idly.

Freed scowled mildly and flicked the toothpick away. "I dunno what you're talkin' about," he said indifferently.

Shamrock lazily raised himself on one elbow and looked at Freed. There was no rancor, no hate, no hardness in his eyes—only pity.

"That's just it, Freed," Shamrock said. "You don't know what many people talk about—or what they think, or what's goin' on behind what they say—and do. You don't savvy much. That's why you're where you are."

"What's the matter with where I am?" Freed demanded, almost good-humoredly, for Shamrock's statement was wholly disarmed by his helplessness and apparent innocence.

Shamrock lay back. "I don't mean that. I didn't mean how you stand for money, a job, and such. I meant where you are—now—where you're sittin'."

"And what's the matter with that?" Freed persisted.

Shamrock raised himself and looked at him a long, full ten seconds, then let his head fall back. "Well, you are a sucker," he said softly.

"Well, what is?" Freed said, almost truculently.

Shamrock yawned, then laughed a little. "Why ain't somebody else—one of the posse, say—sittin' there in that chair instead of you, Freed?"

"Why?" Freed said, and laughed shortly. "Why, I know just when to quit fightin'. When they git in the cell here, I'll give up. Maybe some other hand wouldn't know how to do it right."

"Yeah. Sure," Shamrock said, a little note of jeering in his voice.

"Well, why, then?"

"Oh, let it go," Shamrock said, and added, "Hell, you've done nothin' to me but try to put slugs in my back. Why should I tell you?"

Freed was quiet a long time, but Shamrock could see he was worried. Finally he said, "You're loco."

"Sure," Shamrock agreed. "Still, I got sense enough to pull in my head when somebody tries to knock it off."

He let Freed chew on that a bit while he listened to the sounds. There were many people close to the jail now, and once in a while he could hear a shout. Men in the office were answering, but he could not make out through the thick steel door what they were saying.

"It's comin'," Maginnis said, with a strange calm.

"Yeah," Shamrock replied indifferently, but he was watching Freed, who was listening, too.

Suddenly Freed looked at him and said, "I don't know what your game is, you, but keep your mouth shut. Savvy?"

Hyatt, who had been listening all the while, suddenly laughed. "Let him go, Ireland. Why do him the favor?"

"Yeah. Why?"

Freed squirmed uncomfortably in his seat and glared at them, but his curiosity was definitely aroused, and Shamrock, content with that, remained silent.

Freed tried to settle back into placidity, but he sensed the others were watching him, Shamrock with a kind of superior pity that was more rankling than speech.

"What favor?" Freed said suddenly. Shamrock had to go back and recall what had been said, the wait had been so long. At that moment, a lone rifle shot cracked out in the street, and the crowd yelled. Freed seemingly did not hear it.

"Never mind. It's too late now, I reckon," Shamrock drawled.

Freed got to his feet. "What in *hell* are you talkin' about?" he demanded truculently of Shamrock, then, when Shamrock did not answer, he looked at Hyatt and Maginnis.

"Sit down," Hyatt said in a kindly voice. "We're not

cryin'. Take your medicine."

It was this final jibe that served as the goad to Freed. He swung his shotgun up menacingly.

"I've taken enough rawhidin' from you two. Shut up!" Then, when none of them moved, nor spoke, nor paid any attention to him, his gun sagged. He studied them all, but Shamrock especially.

"What is it?" Freed demanded bluntly. "Say it out, you. What are you talkin' about—the lot of you?"

Shamrock deliberately raised himself on his elbow and looked at Freed. "You damn fool," he said softly, without heat. "You poor damned fool. All we're tryin' to tell you is that you're goin' to get it, too—right along with us. *You're goin' to get killed.* There. Is that plain enough? Now sit down and quit belly-achin'."

He flopped back on the cot and stared at the ceiling. Freed walked slowly over to his cell and looked in. Then he laughed, long and loud, but his eyes were uneasy, and his laughter was a little forced. It died on a false note when nobody smiled, and when all he got was looks of pity.

Shamrock took his Durham sack and held it out to Freed.

"Here. Roll a smoke. If we're lucky, they'll get it over with in a hurry."

Freed ignored the sack and looked at Shamrock. "What the hell ever gave you that idea?"

"What idea?"

"About my gettin' it. You tryin' to spook me?"

"No," Shamrock said indifferently. "I just know, that's all."

"How?"

Lazily, Shamrock rolled over and took off the money belt which Lobell had forgotten to take off him. He pulled out the double eagles and laid them in twin piles. "Five hundred," he said, pointing to one and looking at Freed.

"That was to serve the paper on Hyatt—or kill him if I could." He pointed to the other pile. "That was to kill five of you—Soholt, Harmer, Pace, Coyne, and you."

Freed, attentive, said huskily, "You lie."

"All right. Let it ride. I lie."

"Who paid you? Not—not—"

"Lobell, the old curly wolf," Shamrock drawled lazily. "Who do you think? A hundred dollars a head to get rid of his crew."

"Why? Why'd he want to?" Freed asked, after a long pause.

"For different reasons, but they all amount to the same thing. Do you think he'd let five men live that knew as much about him as you did?"

"You lie!" Freed said.

"Do I? What happened to Soholt, Coyne, Pace? Why do you think I killed Soholt?"

"He saw your reward poster and tried to collect bounty."

"And who showed him the poster?"

Freed said nothing, and Shamrock smiled.

"Lobell did. Do you know why? Do you know his special reason for wantin' Soholt dead? I'll tell you. It was because Soholt had the brains to see that the man that got the Double Diamond held the aces. He sold out to Gillespie. Gillespie was aimin' to get rid of Lobell as soon as Lobell laid the Double Diamond in his hands, and he hired Soholt to do it. Lobell guessed it." He laughed harshly. "He framed Soholt—told him about me and told him to collect the bounty. Soholt picked a fight with me and I killed him, leavin' me clear. Hell, there weren't even slugs in Soholt's shells."

Freed was watching him steadily, his face still, alert for once.

"Lobell and me had it rigged to get Coyne and Pace there at the stables that night," Shamrock continued.

"That was an accident," Freed blurted out.

"Was it?" Shamrock asked softly. "Maybe it looked that way. I shoved Coyne in the middle, so the bunch of you cut down on him. When the shootin' started, I was s'posed to cut down on Pace." He paused, then said, "Remember Lobell bein' so careful to tell Pace where to stand?"

Freed did remember, and it showed on his face.

"But I didn't do it. I wanted more money. That's what Lobell was so proddy about. We went over to the saloon and talked it over. Lobell began to suspect I was double-crossin' him then, but he wasn't sure. I was. He had it framed for me to gun you and Pace at the jail that night. I never did it. I went in and got the keys. The next day he didn't know where he stood, but when he saw that Hyatt was leavin' without a fight, he knew he had to get rid of his gunmen. So he cut down on Pace on the way back."

"Pace was crooked. Lobell said so."

"And you know he wasn't, don't you?" Shamrock said bluntly. "When we got back to town and Hyatt hadn't been there, he was sure I was crossin' him. Then he had to go careful with you because he needed you to fight me and Hyatt." He spread his hands expressively and leaned back against the wall, watching Freed.

Freed stood leaning against the opposite cell, his loose face still, thinking laboriously. Hyatt and Maginnis were utterly quiet.

"There ain't many of you left that can give him away," Shamrock said. "Them two Texans are dead. Harmer and George will be in the mob tonight. You'll be in here. And Lobell will take care of you all tonight. If some saddle tramp in that mob out there that he's picked up in the saloon and paid don't gun you tonight, Freed, Lobell will himself. In all this gunplay, the lot of you will get killed." He smiled indulgently and drew out his Durham sack.

"After tonight, he's a free man. His back trail is blanked

out. You're dead, Harmer's dead, George is dead, we're all dead. There. That easy to savvy?"

He rolled a smoke and lighted it, then drew his legs up on the cot and watched Freed. It was out, the whole gigantic fraud, and he had to admit that it had sounded convincing. The rattle of gunfire was steady now. Probably the warning shots from the sheriff's office were over, and Scott had got down to defending it.

Freed was standing utterly still, his face working, his mouth forming words which he never uttered. Hyatt was quiet, almost afraid to move. The sound of Maginnis's breathing came plain.

"You're trapped, Freed," Shamrock said softly. "You'll never get out now. Listen to that gunfire. It won't be long before they rush the office. The men out there will surrender, but they won't let you. Someone will shoot you—by accident. Funny, isn't it?"

Freed slid a look at the closed corridor door, then licked his lips.

"Roll a smoke and sit down," Shamrock said. "They've got us."

Then Freed began to speak. A torrent of obscenity, curses, oaths, threats poured from his mouth, all directed at Lobell. His hands gripped the shotgun until they were white. All the judgment that he should have called up to sift Shamrock's evidence was swept away by his anger.

"I've gotta get outa here," he finished hoarsely. "I don't give a damn if they kill me. I'm goin' to get Lobell! I've got to get him!"

"You can't," Shamrock said. "We're cornered."

"Then I'll fight that damned mob until they have to dynamite the jail down on me."

"You can't see two ways," Shamrock pointed out. "There's a window here. They'll shoot you through that while you're fightin' the door!"

Freed looked up at the window and cursed again. Then he looked at the cells, at Hyatt, Shamrock, and Maginnis. "Will you help me?"

Shamrock was long in answering, as if he were weighing their chances of success. Finally, he rose. "Well, I'd rather die with a gun in my hand than swingin' from a rope. Sure I will."

Freed leaped for the keys, and Hyatt shot a mute look of gratitude at Shamrock.

Freed was in such haste that he took an inordinate time to open the cells, but finally the three of them stepped out into the corridor.

"Give me a gun," Shamrock said calmly, "one of your six-guns."

Without hesitation, Freed held it out to him.

Calmly, Shamrock took it, stepped back, and leveled it at Freed.

"Sucker," he said, smiling.

CHAPTER EIGHTEEN

FREED TOOK LESS THAN A SECOND to comprehend. Then, in the face of Shamrock's leveled gun, he streaked for his Colt.

Hyatt swung a fast hook that caught Freed behind the ear and stretched him out flat on his face. Maginnis pounced on him like a wildcat and started beating his head with both fists.

Shamrock, laughing, hauled him off.

"Leave off, Lee. He's done us a favor."

Maginnis, his voice choked with great sobs of joy, stepped back.

"I c-can't help it," he said, grinning. "I f-feel so damn

good."

"Rip off his shirt and tie him and gag him, Lee," Shamrock said.

They made short but thorough work of it, then locked Freed in a cell.

Shamrock leaned against the corridor door and looked at Hyatt.

"We aren't out of here yet."

"We'll *git* out," Maginnis said.

"If our luck holds," Hyatt growled. "But how? Listen to that mob. They'll rush the jail before very long. There can't be more than five or six of those men Lobell deputized out in the sheriff's office."

Shamrock looked over their modest armory—two six-guns, a rifle, a shotgun, and a belt of .45 cartridges; then he looked at his companions.

"We can get out of here just one way. By getting Lobell and makin' him confess at the point of a gun."

"He won't do it."

"He's got to do it," Shamrock said.

"But how?"

"I dunno. We'll make him some way."

"But he's not out there in the office. I don't know it, but I can guess."

"I reckon I know where he is," Shamrock said dryly. "He's at the meetin' of the coroner's jury. He's got a jury packed with men that want to see us lynched. As soon as word is brought to him that there's a mob formin', he'll go through the motions of tryin' to leave to stop it. Some bright hombre will draw a gun on him and tell him to sit down. He'll do it, like he couldn't do anything else, and he'll have that alibi."

"But how can you reach him? We're cornered."

"One man can," Shamrock said slowly. "That's all. Just one. The other two will have to stay here and take their chances. Which one will it be? I say Hyatt."

"You," Maginnis said.

"You're elected," Hyatt said. "Now what is it?"

Shamrock explained it briefly and they agreed. Hyatt and Maginnis flattened out against the setbacks on either side of the door out of sight of anyone opening it. Then Shamrock took a six-gun and knocked loudly on the steel door with the butt of it.

The gunfire in the office was a sustained roar now, and he had to knock again and again before he heard the latch click.

The door swung open, and Shamrock dived through the door at a man's throat. The office was dark, and Shamrock, even as he slammed to the floor on top of the man, thanked his luck again. He slashed out with the gun, clubbing savagely as Hyatt and Maginnis swarmed through the door, the latter with the lantern.

"Stick 'em up!" Hyatt roared.

He lay on the floor, out of the sweep of the gunfire coming in the windows, with Maginnis by his side holding the lantern.

The defenders turned, cursing the lantern, to face Hyatt's guns. Scott was there, and when he saw them he cursed bitterly.

"Pile 'em by me—six-guns, too—and I'll blow the light," Hyatt ordered sharply.

Scott was first, for the light was drawing a withering fire from outside. The rest followed suit. Maginnis shoved the guns into the jail, saving one rifle out, then shut the door and leaped to a window. His job was to keep a semblance of defense. Hyatt crowded the men in one corner, then blew out the light. Shamrock had clubbed the sixth man into insensibility. In the dark he spoke to them.

"Can you hear me, Scott?"

"Yes."

"Can a man get out of here?"

Scott laughed. "You'd be cut down before you got ten feet. They're on the roofs across the street and a lot of them are forted up in the stores. You're here to stay, mister."

"Save it," Shamrock said coldly. "Now listen to this. Get it careful, because it's the only way any of you will get out of here alive. Are you listenin'?"

"Yes," Scott said.

"You, Scott," Shamrock said. "This is for you. I'm goin' to crawl in the roll-top desk and have the top rolled down over me. Savvy? Before that we're goin' to scatter coal oil on this floor and start a fire in here—an honest-to-God fire. All of you are goin' to stay in here till she get's roarin', then you, Scott, are goin' to the door and wave your handkerchief. You surrender." He paused, then said, "Got it?"

"So far."

"Good. They'll swarm over here to listen to you. Tell 'em you'll surrender. By that time, this place will be a roarin' hell. The rest of you will be in the jail behind that steel door. Scott, you'll get burned, maybe, but it's better than bein' killed. The jail won't burn because it's adobe. When those men get over here, tell 'em the fire has melted the steel door and they'll have to wait. Then tell them to *get that desk out of here!* Savvy that?"

"I reckon."

"Tell 'em the records are in it—tell 'em anything, only get it hauled out on the street as far as you can from the building. Then forget it. You're free. Is that clear?"

"Plenty."

"You're wonderin' what I aim to do, Scott, and I'll tell you. I'm goin' to get the man that can prove we're innocent!" He paused a moment, letting that sink in. "As soon as these other men get in the jail, Maginnis and Hyatt will surrender to them. They're honest men, aren't they, Scott?"

"If I am, they are."

"Good. You'll be losin' nothin' that way, Scott. Your men will have Hyatt. The only difference will be that I'll have the chance to prove we're innocent."

"And escape."

"That's a lie, Scott," Shamrock said calmly. "You know it is. If I wanted to run out on Hyatt and Maginnis before, I could have done it."

"I reckon you could, at that," Scott admitted.

"There won't be a gun on you, Scott—nothin' to force you to do all this—except your word that you'll go through with it. Will you give it?"

"No," Scott answered promptly.

"All right, then. You'll die with us," Shamrock said coldly.

Scott was silent a moment. Maginnis was keeping up a steady motion of firing and ducking, and he was successfully drawing the fire from the attackers.

"How do you expect a man to keep his word when you threaten him with death if he doesn't give it?" Scott said.

"Have I threatened you?" Shamrock asked. "Make up your mind. If you say no, I'll give you your guns, and we'll fight till they take us." He hesitated a moment. "Look here, Scott. All we're askin' is a chance to prove our innocence. No one can do it for us. You'll lose nothin'."

"Do it, Scott," one of the men growled. "He sounds like he knows what he's talkin' about."

"All right," Scott said. "I'll do it. You deserve that, anyway."

"That's nice of you," Shamrock said dryly. "Let's go. Scott, you come out of there."

Shamrock broke the lantern, unscrewed the cap, and sloshed coal oil over the floor. Scott found the office lamp, a bigger one, and the wastebasket. They broke the chairs for kindling, sloshed the walls with coal oil, soaked the paper, covered the room. Shamrock swept the desk free of litter to make room for him. When he was done, he strapped on a gun belt and took a six-gun. Then he crawled over to Maginnis.

"Good luck, kid," he muttered. "They haven't got us yet."

"Good luck," Lee said hoarsely.

Shamrock crawled over to the desk.

"Turn the back against the wall," he said. "I'll have less chance of gettin' a slug."

"It's suicide, man," Scott said. "You'll never make it."

"Maybe not," Shamrock conceded shortly, and crawled up on the desk. He hunched up, and Hyatt pulled the cover down. It was a tight fit, and Shamrock had to kick out one of the compartments for his feet. As it closed on him, he held the six-gun folded over his chest, its barrel against the lock which he would have to shoot off to get out, since the top locked automatically.

Hyatt turned to Scott. "Are you ready?"

"You're fools," Scott said. "It'll never work—but I hope it does."

Hyatt ordered Maginnis to cease firing, and he herded the others into the jail. When he and Scott were alone, he said to Scott, "Stay as long as you can. That's part of the bargain."

Then he, too, went into the jail, and Scott closed the door behind him. Scott crawled over to the kerosene-soaked pile of litter in the middle of the floor and touched it off with a match. Then he lay on the floor and crawled over to the door and opened it a bit. It seemed as if it took only seconds for the whole room to turn into an inferno. The walls, floor, and ceiling were dried out with the sun and heat of years, and with the aid of the kerosene, they seemed almost to explode into flame. Only the spaces occupied by the desk and by Scott himself were not ablaze.

Scott buried his face in his arms and lay there, listening. He could not be certain, but he thought the firing had ceased. His feet were getting hot and he drew them to him. Only once did he look up for a second, and he saw that the floor in front of the corridor door was sending a solid sheet of flame up the door. He buried his head again, choking and gasping, to wait longer. His clothes were so hot they seared his flesh where they touched. Then he heard the roof timbers crack, and he knew he must get out.

He whipped out his handkerchief, threw the door open, and stood on the steps. Already a few of the hardier souls were advancing to the middle of the street.

Now they came running in twos and threes from the stores across the street.

Scott stood coughing and choking on the steps. When one of them went to go in, he barred the way.

"Stay out! It's hell in there!"

"What happened?"

"The lamp tipped over."

"Where are the others?"

"Dead," Scott lied. "A bullet creased me and when I come to the place was on fire." There was a smoking patch of cloth on his arm and he batted it out, looking over the men.

"Where's Hyatt?"

"He's safe," Scott said bitterly. "You'll have to wait till the fires dies, though. You'll never make it to that door."

"We'll wait," one man said grimly.

Suddenly Scott whirled and involuntarily took a step toward the room.

"The desk!" he yelled. "All the evidence against Hyatt —the keys, the gun—are locked in the desk!"

"Let it go!" One man laughed. "Hell, we don't need evidence."

Scott whirled to face the speaker. "You damned fool.

Don't you know the Governor paroled Hyatt? He might excuse this lynchin' if he was to see the evidence, but if he don't, there'll be hell to pay. They'll close all this free range on us just for a lesson."

Put thus, the men in the front row of the mob considered.

"I'm goin' in," Scott said. "Who'll go with me?"

Two other men volunteered, and Scott tied a handkerchief around his face and dived into the room. The desk, he saw, was starting to burn. The heat was unbearable, for the walls, the floor, the roof, everything was blazing. Only one corner behind the desk was not yet afire. Scott lunged for this corner, braced his feet against the wall, and shoved the desk. It put the far end of the desk close enough to the door so that the two volunteers who had been hanging back in fear of the flames battled their way in and grabbed it.

The floor under Scott was aflame and the desk was heavy, and when he lifted it, it seemed to him that the floor gave. His feet were being burned, the desk needed two men to lift it, but he worked savagely at it, his hands scorching, his breath hot agony.

Slowly, slowly it went out through the door, paused on the steps, and with a last mighty heave it was on the boardwalk. The mob was gathered around the jail now. Scott, coughing, leaned against the desk, hiding his burned hands by clenching his fists.

"Let's get this out of the way," he said casually to the men in the fore of the circle.

Several of the men stepped up, and the desk was moved through the crowd out in the street almost to the alley. Scott wondered if they would wait for it to be opened, but they all turned back to the fire to watch it. Scott stayed back and waited a moment, beating out the last flames on the legs of the desk. When the attention of the crowd was again drawn to the fire, he knocked on the desk.

Shamrock answered, and Scott stepped out of the way. Then a muffled shot sounded. Only a few persons at the very rear of the crowd—women mostly—looked at the desk, but its back was to them and they could see nothing.

Then the top rolled up, and Shamrock turned over and fell out. He was coughing, gagging, and his shot had set his shirt sleeve on fire, but he slapped it out, squatting in the shelter of the desk, fighting to get his breath.

"They're not lookin'," Scott said.

"Much obliged," Shamrock said.

"I'm goin' with you," Scott said grimly.

"Come on, then."

Shamrock stood up, looked around at the burning building, which was a solid pillar of flame now, and raced for the alley across the street. Scott was behind him. In the shadow of the alley, Shamrock made straight for the rear of the hotel.

He paused at its corner. "Give me a boost."

"Where?"

"The roof of this building."

"What do you—?"

"Don't talk, man! Do it!"

Even though his hands were burned, Scott made a step up with them for Shamrock's foot.

Once up, Shamrock said, "You comin'?"

"Yes."

"Then throw that gun down."

"No."

"Fella," Shamrock said coldly, "I haven't got time to argue. Unload and come up or keep it and stay down. Raise the town if you want. I don't care—only do somethin'."

"Damn you!" Scott said, and flipped his gun to the ground. Shamrock reached down and swung him up.

They made their way back along the eaves for forty feet or so, then Shamrock repeated, "Give me a boost."

Scott, his teeth set, boosted him up the sloping roof of the hotel. It was a precarious position, for the shingles were slippery, but Shamrock braced his feet on the solid eaves-trough, unbuckled his gun belt, and let it down. Scott, grim-lipped, pulled himself up, and with Shamrock's help swung up onto the roof.

Then Shamrock took off his boots.

"If you get in my way now, Scott, I'll let you have it. I mean that. I'm not killin', but there may be gunplay and it may look funny. But keep away from me."

"All right," Scott said.

Then Shamrock turned. Above him, the gabled window of Gillespie's room showed plainly. He could picture the coroner's jury holding Lobell there, and he could imagine the sheriff's mild protests. He thanked his luck again that the window was not on the other slope of the roof, so the men in the room would be watching the fire. Slowly he started up on the slippery shingles. It was slow, cautious work, but foot by foot he clawed up the roof.

At last he reached the sill, and he laid a hand on it to hold him while Scott sweated up after him. When Scott had a hand on the sill, Shamrock forgot him. He raised himself up and looked in the window.

CHAPTER NINETEEN

THERE SAT LOBELL at the far end of the room in the same chair where Gillespie had been killed. By him was the table, with the lamp on it. A group of men were scattered throughout the room, but the man on the cot next to

Lobell held a gun. It was pointed at the sheriff.

Shamrock pulled himself through the window and palmed his gun up hip-high.

"Drop it!" he said to the man on the bed.

Every man in the room started at the voice. Shamrock didn't bother to look at Lobell's face. He was watching the gun. When it started its arc toward him, he shot.

The gun slammed out of the man's hand and dropped to the floor.

"The first man in this room that moves is goin' to get killed," Shamrock said flatly, unequivocally.

Then he looked at Lobell. The sheriff's features were composed, no surprise in them, only a look of cunning.

"Well, well," the sheriff drawled amiably. "You take a lot of killin', don't you?"

Shamrock took two steps forward. Scott was behind him, but he had Scott's word. He smiled a little at Lobell.

"Recite your piece, Pop," he sneered. "Then listen. Freed gave you away—dead away. I bought him off with the thousand bucks you gave me to kill Hyatt."

Lobell's face did not change but he looked at Scott.

"Scott heard it," Shamrock lied. "The whole works—every bit of it."

Lobell's gaze searched Shamrock's face, his eyes, but he could read nothing in that still, cold face. Scott, wise man, kept silent.

"You want to hear it?" Shamrock jeered. "He told how you turned that lynch mob on old Maginnis—just like you did on us tonight—after you killed Dick Hyatt. He told about the gold old Maginnis had discovered over the mountain, gold that you and Gillespie killed him for. He told about the water you need—the Double Diamond water you needed to siphon over for placer minin'—that you killed Dick Hyatt for and rustled his spread into the bank's hands. He told about your killin' Gillespie and throwin' the blame on Hyatt—about your tryin' to kill young Maginnis because he could give the game away." He paused, watching Lobell's face. "He even told how you planned to kill Nancy Hyatt because she'd be the only person left alive that could give you away."

"Prove it!" Lobell said, and his voice was strangely hoarse. It was Scott, standing there silently by Shamrock, that was so convincing, that raised the doubt in the sheriff's mind. That, and the fact that Shamrock was free and had a gun.

"I'm goin' to let Freed do that," Shamrock said softly. "The mob's down there now, gettin' the whole story from him. They'll want to see you, Pop."

Lobell's facial muscles moved just a little, and Shamrock saw it coming.

"Better come along, Pop. They want to hear you."

It was the mention of the mob that did it. Even as Shamrock ceased speaking, a roar welled up from the mob. Perhaps the roof had fallen. Shamrock laughed and jerked his head.

"Hear them?"

Then Lobell exploded. With a sweep of his arm, he knocked the lamp off the table and threw the room into darkness. Shamrock fell flat on his face, uncocking his gun. Three swift shots slammed into the wall behind him— Lobell's shots. The room was a madhouse. Shamrock heard someone crash into the stove, and the pipe clattered down.

"The door!" Shamrock roared. "Watch the door for him!"

Then he lay there, grinning, watching the window. Men were cursing, afraid to shoot, afraid for their own lives, and wild with panic.

When Shamrock saw a figure bolt to the window and out of it, he rammed his gun in his belt and fought through to the opening. He had seen enough. The man who went through had not slid down the roof. Only Lobell, thinking Shamrock was watching the door for him, would think that fast.

Shamrock swung up through the window, and crawled slowly up the shingles. Lobell couldn't get down on the other side unless he moved up front, because the adjoining building was short.

Shamrock saw something move on the ridgepole, saw a big bulk crawling along it, but he did not draw his gun.

When he achieved the ridge, he saw Lobell ahead of him, his form outlined by the light of the fire. Shamrock laughed softly, stood up, and started walking along the ridge toward the front of the hotel. Lobell had not even looked back.

Then Shamrock sensed what he was doing. The big false front of the hotel loomed square before them. Lobell would reach it, work down the roof slope to where the false front of the adjoining building—much lower—nearly met the eaves of the hotel. A jump to that false front, twenty feet along it, and he would reach the ridge of that roof. He could slide down the far side of it with only a ten-foot drop to the ground.

Softly Shamrock followed him, losing sight of him now and then, but picking him up again.

They were close to the false front. Shamrock let his hand fall to his belt. When Lobell reached the false front, he stood up, so that he was silhouetted plainly against the light coming up from the street.

He turned to look back.

Then Shamrock laughed harshly. He had come up in his stocking feet so that only twenty feet remained between him and the sheriff.

"Fill your hand, Pop," he said gently out of the night. "It's trail's end!"

With an oath, Lobell streaked for his gun, but Shamrock's hand was already on the downswing.

He whipped out his Colt with a savage laugh in a close, swiveling arc and shot.

The first shot caught Lobell in the side and twisted him. The second drove him a step back along the ridge but he had his gun clear now and he shot.

The third sent him back another step and he teetered on the edge of the false front.

Then Shamrock let loose his last shot, and it drove Lobell over the edge. A high siren of a scream trailed off and down into the street.

Slowly Shamrock holstered his gun, walked to the edge of the roof, and looked below. There, on the board sidewalk, lay Lobell. Beside him was a black object—maybe a box. Scattered around him were what from that height looked to be leaves of paper.

Shamrock felt something rub his elbow and turned. It was Scott.

"You saw?" Shamrock said.

"I was behind you—saw you go out of the window. Yes. I saw it all."

"Do you believe me?"

"I do," Scott said.

They looked down at the sidewalk, just as the first jury-man burst out of the hotel and stopped short, looking at Lobell.

"Thanks for lyin' for me," Shamrock said briefly.

"Hell, I never lied," Scott said gruffly. "I just kept my mouth shut."

"Let's go down. We've still got Hyatt and Maginnis to get out."

They worked their way down the roof to the eaves where they could step to the false front of the next store. On the far slope of its roof, they dropped to the ground and stepped out onto the street.

Scott said, "Better give me your gun."

Shamrock complied. As they approached, the circle of men gathered about Lobell—mostly jurymen who had come down the stairs—gave way. Shamrock ignored them and walked over to the doctor-coroner kneeling by Lobell.

"Dead?" he asked.

The doctor nodded and stood up. Shamrock looked down at the walk on which the box lay. Banknotes were scattered like autumn leaves around Lobell.

Scott knelt and examined them, then took out the sheaves of banknotes still in the box. The piles near the bottom were scorched. Scott turned the box over and saw that the enamel on the bottom was burned off.

He looked up at Shamrock. "That's the bank money."

"Yes," Shamrock answered tonelessly.

Slowly Scott stood up and addressed the watching men. "Did any of you up in that room hear the stove crash?"

Several of the men nodded.

Scott pointed to the box. "The box was hid in the stove. Lobell must have killed Gillespie, robbed the bank, then come back and hid the loot in the stove—the last place anyone would ever look." He looked down at Lobell, then at the crowd. "Do you understand what we've almost done?"

And without waiting for an answer he said, "Those two in the jail—Maginnis and Hyatt! They're innocent! Come on!"

He raced for the corner, the jurymen with him, leaving Shamrock alone.

CHAPTER TWENTY

THE CROWD had been calmed by its wait, and when Scott and the jurymen came up, it gave way for them. Scott saw Nancy in the crowd and he called her to them. Then the doctor began to speak, talking in a calm tone, prompted occasionally by Nancy, telling them that the sheriff had confessed by his flight, and by the banknotes which he had on him when he was killed. He was ringed by the jurymen. All the while he was talking, the timbers of the office were burning themselves out, and the crowd listened earnestly.

Shamrock heard part of it from the corner, and when he was certain that the mob would listen, he skirted the crowd and headed toward the stables. He flattened himself against a store, watching.

It was Harmer that broke through first, and he started for the stables. Shamrock stepped out of the shadow beside him, gun in hand.

"Want to get lynched?" he drawled.

"Don't say anything!" Harmer pleaded hoarsely, looking back at the listening mob only a few feet away. "I'll go—anywhere." Shamrock took his gun and together they stepped back into the shadow of the store.

George was the second, and when he was free of the crowd, he began to run for the stables when Shamrock's drawl hauled him up short.

"You too, mister."

George stopped on the sidewalk and looked at Shamrock and Harmer. He stood utterly still, six feet away, staring.

"Will you take it from me or from the mob?" Shamrock

asked.

"I—I give up," George said hoarsely. "Only don't let that mob touch me!"

"Come over here."

George stepped into the doorway and Shamrock disarmed him. Then they watched the mob, listening to the doctor. Suddenly a murmur ran through the crowd, followed by a few hoarse cheers.

Then the mob broke and four men ran across the street to a store. In a moment they returned with shovels and crowbars. The crowd cheered them, but this time there was a different note in the mass voice, a note of applause, of relaxed tension, of praise.

The doctor and Scott and Nancy had conquered.

Shamrock smiled a little. To Harmer he said, "Go tell one of those kids on the edge to bring Scott over to the hotel."

"What if they—" Harmer began, but Shamrock prodded him out onto the sidewalk.

Furtively Harmer spoke to a boy who had been listening to the talk. Shamrock saw Harmer slip him some money and saw the boy disappear.

When Harmer had returned, Shamrock said, "We're goin' to the hotel."

"But they'll see us!" Harmer pleaded.

"If they do, that's tough. But I don't think they will. They'll be too busy watchin' the jail. Now step out. Walk straight, you two coyotes. I'm right behind you."

Side by side, Harmer and George stepped out and walked around the crowd. Shamrock, hand on gun, fell in behind them. The crowd, as he predicted, was busy watching a crew of men shovel a path through the glowing embers of the office to the steel door that was just beginning to lose its red-hot color. Not one person turned to see them.

At the hotel, Shamrock sat down in a lobby chair and motioned George and Harmer to seats opposite him. Then he rolled a cigarette, asked Harmer for a match, got it, lighted his smoke, and sat back with a weary sigh of satisfaction.

Scott wasn't alone when he came. Hyatt, Maginnis, Nancy, and a dozen of the older ranchers were with him when he entered the lobby.

Shamrock smiled when he saw Maginnis, grimed and cheerful, and Hyatt, his face serene and happy.

Scott smiled, too, when he saw Harmer and George. Shamrock was standing now, and he indicated the two.

"That cleans it up. They'll tell you what you want to know."

Firmly, but gently, Scott shoved Shamrock back into his seat, while the others drew up chairs or stood around them. Shamrock looked curiously from one to the other.

"This is a mass meetin' of the big ranchers of Jicarilla County, Ireland," he announced by way of explanation.

Shamrock nodded wearily. They were sober, substantial-looking men, who studied him with quiet regard.

"Maybe I can speak for them," Scott said, suddenly sober. He looked at Hyatt. "We've been damn fools, Mayo. The lot of us. We're behind you now to a man."

Then he turned to Shamrock. "We want to put you in office to serve out the rest of Lobell's term—after which we hope you'll take it again."

Shamrock shook his head and looked uncomfortable.

"Will you take it?"

"Thanks. I reckon not."

"Why not?"

"I—I can't," Shamrock said.

"Why not?"

"Well, I—I can't, that's all. I'm hittin' the trail tonight."

"Is it that marshal in Montana?" Scott asked suddenly.

Shamrock looked over the group warily, then nodded.

"Was it a fair fight?" Scott asked.

Shamrock's eyes chilled. "He cold-decked me, then when I caught him, he accused me of it and went for his gun."

"Any witnesses?"

"Plenty."

Scott scowled. "Why did you run, then?"

"I was sick of the place," Shamrock said. "I wanted to hit the trail. I didn't want to stop to argue it out."

Scott turned to the men in the group. "We can petition the governor not to honor the extradition papers until all witnesses are accounted for and their stories recorded, can't we? Remember, it's only a town marshal, so the Federal government won't step in."

"He was a deputy U.S. marshal," Shamrock said.

Scott turned to him. "Who said so?"

"Lobell."

Scott laughed softly. "I reckon that's the only thing he ever said you didn't doubt, Ireland. The poster was in the drawer of the desk—filed, for future reference. It offered a thousand reward for you. You killed a town marshal."

Shamrock cursed softly.

"We don't propose to be cheated out of a sheriff by a crooked accusation like that," Scott said with grim good humor. "There isn't a man in this crowd that's got the sense he was born with, or this wouldn't have happened. From now on, we watch our sheriffs—beginnin' with you, Ireland. Will you take it?"

"Pay him what he wants," one of the ranchers said. "Let him make his own terms."

"Better take it, son," another man said. "We like what we've seen of you." He laughed and looked at the other men. "If you turn us down, we'll ship you right back to Montana to face that charge."

Shamrock looked at Hyatt and Nancy. They both nodded, urging him to do it.

"You don't know anything about me," he protested.

"All we want," Scott said. "Will you take it?"

"All right—after I go up and clear my name, I'll be back to try it."

"Good," Scott said, rising. He slipped something into Shamrock's hand—the star of the sheriff's office. "Take that with you—Sheriff."

Shamrock's first duty was to lock Freed, Harmer, and George in jail. Maginnis and Hyatt went with him. The crowd had gone about their business.

As they shut the steel door and stepped out in the ashes, Hyatt said, "Now let's eat. Nancy's got a meal ordered at the hotel."

"You go up," Shamrock said. "I'll go see about Blue, then I'll be with you."

Hyatt and Maginnis left, while he walked down to the stables. His hand was on the star in his pocket, and some bottomless pessimism told him it wouldn't work.

He stepped in the door of the stable. The lantern was lighted, and he walked back to Blue's stall.

As he turned into it, he saw something move at Blue's head.

"Who's that?"

"Nancy." She came out and handed him a slip of paper. "I was looking through the box of Lobell's. I found this."

"What is it?"

"The map to Lee's gold—the location of it."

Shamrock accepted it in silence, and put it in his pocket, aware that Nancy was watching him.

"How long will it take to get to Montana?" she asked.

"A month, six weeks."

"I'm sure it will be all right," Nancy said gently.

"You are?" Shamrock asked slowly. "I wish I was. Why

are you?"

"Lots of reasons. Your face, for one."

Shamrock only scowled. "What's my face got to do with it?"

"When you rode in here, all a man had to do to get mad was look at you. That's not so now."

"I won't get by on my face, changed or not."

"You'll get by on something else," Nancy said softly. "Have you ever had men behind you?"

"Plenty of times," Shamrock said dryly. "Chasing me."

Nancy laughed. "I didn't mean that, and you know it. I mean have you ever had the friendship of men in the community?"

"No."

"You have now."

"Only men?" Shamrock asked.

"We'll talk about that when you're back from Montana."